Dante's Inferno: A Retelling in Prose

David Bruce

Published by David Bruce, 2022.

DANTE'S INFERNO: A RETELLING IN PROSE

First edition. July 4, 2022.

ISBN: 979-8201476052

Written by David Bruce.

Table of Contents

Dedication

Dedicated to Carl Eugene Bruce and Josephine Saturday Bruce

My father, Carl Eugene Bruce, died on 24 October 2013. He used to work for Ohio Power, and at one time, his job was to shut off the electricity of people who had not paid their bills. He sometimes would find a home with an impoverished mother and some children. Instead of shutting off their electricity, he would tell the mother that she needed to pay her bill or soon her electricity would be shut off. He would write on a form that no one was home when he stopped by because if no one was home he did not have to shut off their electricity.

The best good deed that anyone ever did for my father occurred after a storm that knocked down many power lines. He and other linemen worked long hours and got wet and cold. Their feet were freezing because water got into their boots and soaked their socks. Fortunately, a kind woman gave my father and the other linemen dry socks to wear.

My mother, Josephine Saturday Bruce, died on 14 June 2003. She used to work at a store that sold clothing. One day, an impoverished mother with a baby clothed in rags walked into the store and started shoplifting in an interesting way: The mother took the rags off her baby and dressed the infant in new clothing. My mother knew that this mother could not afford to buy the clothing, but she helped the mother dress her baby and then she watched as the mother walked out of the store without paying.

My mother and my father both died at 7:40 p.m.

Cover Photograph for Dante's *Inferno*: A Retelling in Prose:
DANTE SCULPTURE IN FLORENCE
© Alehnia
Dreamstime.com

***

Educate Yourself
    Read Like A Wolf Eats
    Be Excellent to Each Other
    Books Then, Books Now, Books Forever

***

In this retelling, as in all my retellings, I have tried to make the work of literature accessible to modern readers who may lack the knowledge about mythology, religion, and history that the literary work's contemporary audience had.

Do you know a language other than English? If you do, I give you permission to translate this book, copyright your translation, publish or self-publish it, and keep all the royalties for yourself. (Do give me credit, of course, for the original retelling.)

I would like to see my retellings of classic literature used in schools, so I give permission to the country of Finland (and all other countries) to give copies of any or all of my retellings to all students forever. I also give permission to the state of Texas (and all other states) to give copies of this book to all students forever. I also give permission to all teachers to give copies of this book to all students forever.

Teachers need not actually teach my retellings. Teachers are welcome to give students copies of my eBooks as background material. For example, if they are teaching Homer's *Iliad* and *Odyssey*, teachers are welcome to give students copies of my *Virgil's* Aeneid: *A Retelling in Prose* and tell students, "Here's another ancient epic you may want to read in your spare time."

Preface

Contrapasso is divine punishment or divine retribution. It is a punishment that is appropriate for the sin. (Note the word "sin" here instead of "crime." Not all sins are crimes. It is not against the law to be a glutton.)

If you are unfamiliar with Dante and *The Divine Comedy*, you may want to read the Background Information near the end first.

Chapter 1: The Dark Wood of Error

Just before Good Friday, April 8, 1300, Dante woke up to find himself in a dark wood. How he got there he did not know because he had wandered from the correct path little by little, not realizing for a long time that he had wandered from the straight path and was instead on the path of error. But midway in the threescore and ten years allotted to human beings in the Bible, the 35-year-old Dante had finally awoken to find out that he was not on the path he wanted to be on. Instead, he was in a dark wood in a dark valley, far from the light he wanted to see. And he felt fear rather than the reassurance he wanted to feel.

But Dante looked up and saw the light shining on the top of a hill. Light shows human beings the correct path to take, and light calms fears. A swimmer who has escaped dangerous waters will take a look at the waters when he is safe on shore. So Dante, who felt safer but still had a long way to go before he reached the light, looked at the dark path and the dark valley while resting before he attempted to climb the hill and reach the light.

The climb was harder than he expected because of Dante's weakness — one foot dragged behind the other. Worse, Dante was not alone. Just as he began the climb upward, a leopard blocked his path. Everywhere Dante went, the leopard went. Dante was unable to climb upward. Just when Dante thought that he could get past the leopard, a lion appeared and blocked his path. And then still more trouble! A she-wolf appeared, and again Dante's path upward was blocked. Dante was unable to climb upward; instead, the she-wolf, hungry, walked toward him, forcing him down the hill into the dark wood and the dark valley.

If Dante were to ever climb upward, he needed help. Some things cannot be accomplished alone. Some things require help to be accomplished, and some things require divine help to be accomplished.

Just then, Dante saw a figure coming toward him, and he cried out, "Whoever you are, have pity on me, whether you are a man or a spirit!"

The figure replied, "I am no longer a living man, although I lived in Rome while Caesar Augustus ruled, in a time when the wrong gods were worshipped. I was a poet, and as a poet I told the story of Aeneas, a refugee who survived the burning of Troy. But why aren't you climbing toward the light? This dark wood is no place to be."

I know why you can't climb toward the light, the figure — Virgil — thought. *You have sinned, and you are in the dark wood of error. Your sins are keeping you from climbing toward the light. The leopard is a manifestation of the sins of incontinence, the lion is a manifestation of the sins of violence, and the she-wolf is a manifestation of the sins of fraud. Sometimes, sins take on material form. Dante, I am aware that you have messed up your life so much that you need help to reach the light. Fortunately for you, help is here.*

"Are you Virgil, author of the *Aeneid*? Can you now help me, who have spent so much time studying and adoring your poetry?" Dante asked. "You, Virgil, taught me to write poetry. You, Virgil, taught me the style that has been so much admired. A beast has kept me from climbing to the light. Save me from the beast!"

"I can help you to go further toward the light," Virgil replied, "but we must go in another direction. The beast that keeps you from climbing the hill and reaching the light allows no one to get past her. She always blocks travelers. This she has always done and will continue to do until a champion arises to slay her. Such a champion will not be concerned with money or property, but will concern himself with wisdom, love, excellence, and virtue. The beast will not survive the encounter with the champion.

"But follow me. I will be your guide, and I will take you most of the way through your journey. First we shall visit a place of screams, and then we shall visit a place where souls rejoice in what may seem like punishment because they know that they shall reach Paradise. I shall take you as far as I can, and then a soul worthier than I am shall take you the rest of the way to your destination. I cannot take you that far because I did not worship the Supreme Emperor in the right way. The Supreme Emperor is the ruler of everything, and all of his citizens are happy."

"Poet," Dante begged, "in the name of that God Whom you did not worship rightly, please save me from this dark wood. Lead me to the place you mention, and let me see the gate that Saint Peter guards."

Virgil led the way, and Dante followed him.

Chapter 2: Dante Hesitates

The night began to fall, and although most men were preparing for bed and sleep, Dante was preparing for a rough journey in which he would battle the pity that he could so easily feel for other people. To tell this journey later, he would require the help of the Muses.

Dante was troubled. He said to Virgil, "Tell me if you think that I am able to undertake this journey. You wrote about Aeneas, who visited the Land of the Dead while he was still living. He deserved such special consideration because of who he is: the founder of the Roman people. And Rome became not just the center of an empire, but also the residence of the Popes. Aeneas learned much in the Land of the Dead — much that would help him as he fought to establish himself in Italy and to create the people who would found Rome and the papal seat.

"Another person who visited the Land of the Dead is Saint Paul, as we read in the *Visio Sancti Pauli*. He brought back from the Land of the Dead confirmation of the Christian faith.

"But who am I to make such a journey? I am not Aeneas. I am not Saint Paul. I do not think that I am worthy to undertake such a journey, and I cannot believe that any other man would think that I am worthy of undertaking it.

"But what do *you* think? You are wise."

Dante was having second thoughts, and no wonder. This journey was not through pleasant country. This was not a journey of a tourist. Instead, this was a journey through a land of screams.

"A great journey is ahead of you," Virgil replied, "yet you are shying away from it like a coward or an animal that is afraid of its own shadow. To put courage in your heart, let me explain why I am here. Let me explain the pity I felt when I learned that you had strayed from the path of truth and had found yourself in the dark wood of error.

"I was in Limbo with the other souls who deserve neither torture nor bliss. A beautiful and blessed lady came to me, and I knew immediately that I would do whatever she asked me to do.

"She addressed me, 'Noble poet, who has been, is, and will be famous as long as human beings read poetry, a man has strayed from the path of truth and needs your help, if help is not too late to reach him and guide him. I want you to go and be his guide, and take him through the dark places. My name is Beatrice, and this man loved me while I was alive.'

"'Lady, I will do all that you ask,' I replied, 'but please tell me how you come to be here. Obviously, you come from a much different place, so why are you here in Limbo, the first Circle of Hell?'

"'I have no fear of Limbo, no fear of Hell,' Beatrice told me. 'Once souls are in the place from which I come, souls are incapable of being separated from God and they are incapable of ever feeling the other torments of Hell. The Queen of Heaven helps people in need, and she knows that this man needs help. She called Saint Lucia, to whom this man is devoted, and asked her to find a way to help him. Knowing that this man loved me while I was alive, Saint Lucia came to me and requested, "Beatrice, a man needs help. Can you help the man who loved you so much while you were alive?" I then came to you, and I have asked that you be a guide for this man.'

"And so, Dante, I came quickly to you," Virgil said. "Why are you afraid? Three heavenly ladies — Beatrice, Saint Lucia, and the Queen of Heaven herself — are all looking out for you. With three such champions on your side, what have you to be afraid of?"

The courage rose in Dante just as flowers rise toward sunshine.

"My courage has revived," Dante said. "Beatrice and you are helping me, and I am eager to begin my journey. Let us start at once, as each of us is eager to do. You are my guide, and you are my teacher."

Virgil led the way along a rugged path; Dante followed him.

Chapter 3: The Gate of Hell

They arrived at a gate. Written on the ledge above the gate were these words:

"I am the way to a place of sorrow.

"I am the way to grief that lasts forever.

"I am the way to souls who are forsaken forever.

"Justice moved the creator of this place.

"Divine omnipotence created this place.

"As did Divine omniscience and Divine love.

"Before me only eternal things were made,

"And I am an eternal thing.

"Abandon all of your hopes, all of you who enter."

Dante looked at the words above the gate, and then he said to Virgil, "These words are cruel."

Virgil thought, *This is the beginning of your journey to truth, Dante, and you are still naïve. These words are not cruel. Anyone who is in the Inferno deserves to be here — the Supreme Emperor does not make mistakes.*

Virgil said to Dante, "Be brave now. Trust me, your guide. Now you will begin to see the souls who have lost the good of intellect."

Virgil thought, *Human beings can tell the difference between good and evil. This is something that animals cannot do. A dog does not feel guilty if it eats the food of another dog. Human beings ought to use their intellect to determine the right thing to do and then use their free will to do it. The unrepentant sinners whom Dante will see being punished in the Inferno and outside its gate did not use their intellect and free will to do these things.*

Dante and Virgil heard shrieks piercing the air, and Dante asked Virgil, "Why are these souls grieving?"

Virgil replied, "Outside Hell Proper are the souls of those who never took a stand in life. While living, they were neither for good nor for evil, and now that they are dead, neither Heaven nor Hell wants them. These wretched souls who lived without taking a stand are punished with the angels who remained uncommitted during Lucifer's rebellion against the Supreme Emperor. They did not commit themselves to evil, nor did they commit themselves to good.

Even the souls in Hell feel superior to them because the souls in Hell made a choice: They chose evil."

Dante then asked, "How are these uncommitted souls being punished?"

Virgil replied, "These souls did not truly live, and therefore they will not truly die and go to a final destination, whether Heaven or Hell. Even torment in Hell is preferable to what these souls feel. In addition, these souls did no lasting good or harm on Earth, and they will not be remembered on Earth."

Dante looked at the souls, and he recognized a few of them, but he had no desire to remember or to record their names. They had done nothing to be remembered for, so their names ought to be forgotten.

Dante looked, and he saw their punishment: The souls were never still, for they continually chased a banner that continually moved and never took a stand. As the souls ran, hornets and wasps stung their naked bodies, and their blood and pus and tears ran down their bodies to the maggots on the ground.

Virgil thought, *In life, the uncommitted souls did not follow a banner; in death, they follow a banner endlessly, running after it as it travels here and here, never remaining in one place. Similarly, in life, these noncommitted souls never staked out a firm position. In life, these souls never felt deeply, either for good or for evil. Now, these souls do feel deeply, as hornets and wasps bite them. They bleed from the bites, and maggots eat the pus that flows to the ground. This punishment is fitting. What these souls avoided doing in life, they now do in death. Divine retribution is always deserved, and it is always fitting. Divine retribution is known as* contrapasso.

Dante then looked and saw another group of souls who had gathered at the shore of a river, and he saw that they looked eager for what was about to happen to them, although Dante knew that what was about to happen to them could not be desirable. He asked Virgil, "Who are these souls, and why do they look so eager?"

Virgil replied, "That river is called the Acheron, and I will explain all to you when we reach it."

Dante stayed quiet; he worried that he had been too inquisitive.

Crossing the river in a boat was an aged man who shouted, "Grief is coming for you. No hope of Heaven exists for you. I will take you across the river to a place of darkness, ice, and fire."

Seeing Dante, a living soul, the old man — Charon, the ferryman — thought, *Living souls always bring me trouble. Hercules once came down to the Inferno and carried out of it Cerberus, the three-headed guard dog of Hell. I want no part of a living man in the Inferno.*

He shouted at Dante, "Living soul, go away. Stay away from the dead."

Dante did not move, so Charon added, "You cannot come this way. If you enter the Inferno, you must use a different boat."

Virgil spoke, "Charon, this is not the time for anger. This living soul is here because omnipotent power has sent him here. You need know nothing more."

Virgil's words quieted Charon, but Charon's eyes glowed deep in his eye sockets.

The souls on the riverbank were naked and shivering with fright, remembering what Charon had said about their doom. They were also cursing and blaspheming; they blasphemed God, and they cursed their parents and the day they were born and the entire human species, preferring that the entire human species should never have existed rather than for them to be where they now were. Crying, they waited for Charon's boat to reach the riverbank, and then they boarded the boat as Charon hit with an oar any stragglers. The souls jumped into the boat like leaves falling from trees in autumn.

Virgil explained, "Whenever anyone dies without first having repented, they assemble here no matter where and when they died. They are eager to cross the river, be judged, and be punished, although at the same time they dread it. These souls were eager to sin while they were alive on Earth, so Divine Justice makes them eager for the punishment they so dread. The Supreme Emperor does not make mistakes, and every soul who is punished here deserves that punishment. When Charon makes it clear that he doesn't want you here, it is a compliment."

An earthquake moved the land, and a wind swept the terrain. Dante was so frightened that he fainted.

Chapter 4: Limbo

Thunder sounded, and Dante awoke from his sleep. Charon had already ferried Dante and Virgil across the Acheron, and Dante saw before him the brink of Hell, a deep and dark and hazy place of agonized cries. Dante looked down, but he could see nothing clearly.

Virgil, his face very pale, told Dante, "Let us climb down now. I will go first; follow me."

"You are afraid, Virgil," Dante said. "If you are afraid of this place, how can I descend into it?"

"I am not afraid," Virgil replied. "My face is pale because I feel pity for the souls in Limbo, the first Circle of the Inferno. The color of fear is also the color of pity. Let us go. We have a long journey ahead of us."

Dante and Virgil walked down into the first Circle of Hell. There Dante heard no screams, but only sighs. Grief need not be accompanied by torture. Men, women, and infants were in this Circle.

"You aren't asking me which souls reside here," Virgil said to Dante, "but you ought to know that. It is part of the education you will receive in the Inferno. These souls did not sin, but they deserve to be here nevertheless. Even the souls who did great things while they were alive deserve to be here. Some souls were not baptized while they were alive, and as your faith tells you, baptism opens up Paradise. Or, if the soul lived before Christ was born, the soul did not worship God in the proper way. I myself lived before Christ and failed to worship God in the proper way. For these reasons, these souls — including myself — deserve to be here. We have no hope of ever achieving Paradise, yet we continually desire Paradise."

Dante, like Virgil, pitied the souls here. He asked Virgil, "Have any souls ever left here, either through their own merit or through the help of another?"

Virgil knew the event that Dante was elliptically referring to — the Harrowing of Hell by Christ — and he replied, "I was not long a resident here when a Mighty Warrior came and rescued out of this place such great forebears and Jews as Adam, Abel, Noah, Moses, Abraham, King David, Rachel, and many more. These souls deserved their salvation, and they were the first to be saved of all the souls who have ever existed."

Virgil and Dante continued walking as they talked, traveling through a wood, and Dante saw a fire lighting a residence where honorable souls gathered.

Dante said, "Obviously, this is a special place. Which souls enjoy the honor of residing here?"

"Those souls are still renowned in the living world," Virgil replied. "Their renown above also wins them special honor here."

Dante heard a voice saying, "The renowned poet who left us has returned. Let us greet him."

Four souls began walking toward Virgil and Dante.

Virgil identified them, "The soul in the lead, carrying a sword, is Homer, the mighty author of the *Iliad* and the *Odyssey*, epic poems about the Trojan War and its aftermath. Next is Horace, author of *Satires*, which teaches morality. Then comes Ovid, the author of the *Metamorphoses*, which collected many myths involving metamorphoses or transformations. Finally comes Lucan, the author of the *Pharsalia*, an epic poem about the civil war between Julius Caesar and Pompey the Great."

Together, the group, including Virgil, consisted of the greatest poets of antiquity. By honoring Virgil, the four great poets honored poetry.

The five poets of antiquity talked together briefly, and then they motioned for Dante to join them, an honor that made Virgil smile. And yes, it was a great honor, indeed. Dante's place as a poet is among the greatest poets of all time.

As they talked, they drew near the light. Arriving, they saw a castle circled by seven high walls and by a stream. Dante and the other poets needed no bridge to cross the stream; they walked on water as if they were walking on solid ground.

Passing through seven gates in the seven walls, they arrived at a meadow where renowned souls dwelled. Looking around, Dante recognized many of the souls. He saw heroes and heroines such as Aeneas, the hero of Virgil's *Aeneid* who survived the fall of Troy, took his father and son out of the city (although his wife perished), and led the Trojan survivors to Carthage and then to Italy, where he became the founder of the Roman people. He also saw Lavinia, the Italian princess whom Aeneas married in Italy. She and Aeneas became important ancestors of the Romans. Camilla, a female warrior who fought for the Italians against Aeneas in Italy, was also present.

Among the philosophers whom Dante saw were Democritus, a Greek philosopher who believed in the theory of atoms: the idea that matter is composed of imperishable and indivisible units. Dante also saw Diogenes of Sinope, aka "the Cynic," a Greek philosopher who advocated self-control and abstinence; and he saw Euclid, who is famous for his writing about geometry.

Dante also saw three great Muslims: the philosopher Avicenna, a Persian physician, philosopher, and scientist who memorized the Qur'an; the philosopher Averroës, an Arab who wanted to reconcile Aristotelianism with Islam; and the sultan Saladin, a great Muslim general and leader who captured Jerusalem from the Crusaders.

The Supreme Emperor *is not prejudiced,* Virgil thought, *except against unrepentant sinners. When Muslims deserve a place of honor, and yes, in the Inferno, this castle in Limbo is a place of honor, they get it.*

Virgil led the way once more. Dante followed him, leaving behind the virtuous pagans, and they arrived at a place of darkness.

Chapter 5: The Lustful

Dante and Virgil descended, and they saw Minos, judge of the souls of the damned. Minos is a judge who never errs, but Minos is a monster. He has a long tail, and after he hears a sinner confess his or her sins he wraps his tail around himself to indicate in which Circle of Hell the sinner will be punished. If Minos wraps his tail around himself three times, the sinner will eternally be punished in Circle 3. He then uses his tail to hurl the sinner down closer to where the sinner belongs.

Seeing Dante, Minos said to him, "You have come to an eternal place of pain. Be careful here. Enter carefully, and while you are here, be careful whom you trust. Do not allow anyone to fool you."

Ever cautious, Virgil thought, *Charon the ferryman tried to keep Dante out of the Inferno. Everything that Minos says is wise, but I don't want him to scare Dante — Dante must travel through the Inferno.*

Virgil said to Minos, "Don't try to keep Dante from descending further. This journey is according to the will of the Supreme Emperor. That is all you need to know."

Virgil and Dante passed by Minos, and they began to hear cries in the air. They reached a place of darkness and a storm. The tempestuous winds blow, and as they blow, the sinners caught in its grasp go high or low and from side to side with no control over their speed or position. The tempestuous winds blow them around Circle 2, and whenever they come to the place nearest to Minos, the sinners curse God.

Here in Circle 2 the sinners who are guilty of lust are condemned to eternal torment. These sinners ignored reason and did not control their lust.

Here we see the first of four Circles that punish the incontinent, Virgil thought. *These incontinent sinners gave up the good of intellect in order to give rein to their passion for sin. Instead of using reason to control themselves, they gave up control over themselves and engaged — enthusiastically — in sin.*

Here we see a contrapasso. *These sinners did not want to control themselves and their lust, and here they are not in control of themselves. They do not decide where to go; the tempest winds blow them around the Circle. The sinners control nothing.*

Dante saw many souls, and he asked Virgil, "Who are some of the souls whom I see being blown by the wind?"

Virgil replied, "Semiramis, an Assyrian queen of Babylon, was known for her lechery. She had the laws changed so she could marry her own son.

"Dido is also here. As you know, she had an affair with Aeneas, and when he left her in order to pursue his destiny, she committed suicide."

Virgil thought, *Dido could have appeared in a lower Circle — the Circle devoted to punishing the suicides — but Minos the judge felt that it was more appropriate for her to be punished here. Minos is the perfect judge. The Supreme Emperor chose him, and neither the Supreme Emperor nor Minos makes mistakes.*

Virgil continued, "Paris and Helen of Troy are here. Paris ran off with Helen, the wife of Menelaus. Menelaus and his brother Agamemnon and a Greek army followed the pair to Troy, where the Trojan War was fought to get Helen back for Menelaus.

"Achilles, the Greek hero of the Trojan War, is also here. He fell in love with Polyxena, a daughter of Priam and Hecuba, the Trojan King and Queen, and he agreed to switch sides from the Greeks to the Trojans in order to marry her. However, at the wedding Paris treacherously killed him.

"You also see Cleopatra here. The Queen of Egypt, Cleopatra had love affairs with both Julius Caesar and Mark Antony."

Virgil thought, *Like Dido, Cleopatra committed suicide — she allowed a poisonous snake to bite her — and so Minos could have sentenced her to a lower Circle in Hell, but lust was the greatest of her sins, so Minos sentenced her to eternal punishment in Circle 2.*

Dante then said, "Virgil, I see two souls whom I would like to talk to in particular."

"If you would like to talk to them, you can," Virgil replied. "When they come close, call to them and they will come to you."

When the two souls came close, Dante said, "Souls, if it is not forbidden, please speak to us."

The two souls, male and female, like two doves leaving a flock, left the other souls and descended toward Dante and Virgil.

"O living creature," said the female, addressing Dante.

I know you, Virgil thought. *You are Francesca da Rimini, and you are eloquent and charming. Still, you are where you belong. I know that, and I wish that Dante knew that, but he is still naïve because it is early in his journey.*

If Dante were older and wiser, he would wonder why you called him "O living creature." Dante is a living human being, not a creature. He is not an animal. Why are you referring to him as something that is less than human? I know why.

The sin of incontinence is about rejecting one's humanity. We are humans, not animals, yet humans can rut without having recourse to reason first. Instead of making use of their intellect and free will, the incontinent sinners ignore those things. A human being can use intellect to figure out how much and what kind of sex to engage in, and a continent person uses his or her free will to resist illicit sex and to engage only in consensual and legitimate sex, but an incontinent person ignores his or her humanity and acts like an animal that is incapable of understanding the difference between right and wrong.

A human being can use intellect to know that adultery should be avoided and a human being can use free will to resist the temptation of adultery, but Francesca ignored her own humanity and succumbed to the temptation of committing adultery.

By committing adultery, Francesca did not recognize her own humanity, and by calling Dante a "living creature" rather than a human being, she is not recognizing his humanity.

Reason was not in control of Francesca while she was alive — desire was.

Francesca continued, "You are so gracious and you are so kind. I am honored that you have made your way here to pay us a social call."

Virgil thought, *Why do you think that Dante is paying you a social call? Dante is not in the Inferno specifically to pay a visit to you. He is in the Inferno to discover what he must do to stay out of the Inferno after he is dead. Dante woke up in the dark wood of error, and this journey he is taking is intended to save his soul.*

You think it is all about you, don't you, Francesca? Like many other sinners in the Inferno, you think that you are the center of the universe.

Francesca continued, "If only we were friends with the King of Kings, we would request of Him that He be with you."

Virgil thought, *And why do you say 'if only we were friends with the King of Kings'? Don't you know where you are, Francesca? You are in the Inferno, suffering eternal torment. You will never leave here. Being damned for eternity is not like a little social quarrel that can be fixed with a few eloquent and charming words.*

Francesca continued, "Love conquered this one and made him want the beauty of my body. Love conquered me and made me delight in him who never leaves me. Love led us to be murdered suddenly. The one who murdered us will end up deep in Hell, in Caina."

Interesting, Virgil thought. *You are like most of the sinners in the Inferno. You don't blame yourself. Right now, you are blaming Love. Love — so you think — excuses you from the responsibility of using your reason to figure out right from wrong.*

But you don't really believe that, do you, Francesca? If Love excuses you for committing adultery, that person who murdered you would be excused because he loved you. I know your story, Francesca. I know how you died.

And why are you referring to your partner in sin — the one by your side whom you committed adultery with — as "this one" instead of by his name? I know his name; it is Paolo. You can't stand him now, can you, Francesca? Every time you look at him, you are reminded of why you are in the Inferno. That is part of your eternal punishment, isn't it, Francesca?

Dante was silent for a while, and then Virgil asked him, "What are you thinking about?"

Dante sighed and said, "These two loved each other so much."

Wrong answer, Virgil thought. *Those two sinned, those two did not repent, and those two are exactly where they belong.*

Then Dante turned to the two sinners and said to Francesca, "I pity you because of the torment you are suffering. But how did love lead you to commit the act that got you here?"

Francesca replied, "Remembering the happiness of the past will only increase the unhappiness of the present, but I will tell you. We were reading the tale of Lancelot and his love for the Queen. We were alone, for no one ever suspected us. We read about Lancelot kissing the lips he longed for, and this one by my side kissed me. The book we read was our Galehot. We closed the book, and that day we read no more."

I can't believe that Dante is falling for this rubbish, Virgil thought. *He doesn't know that Francesca is spinning him. She is telling only part of the story. She is leaving out all of the parts that would instantly condemn her. For example, she is leaving out of her story these important facts: 1) She and Paolo are married, but not to each other, 2) She is Paolo's sister-in-law, and 3) Her husband found her and his brother in bed together, and he killed them both.*

In addition, once again Francesca is blaming not herself, but something else. Previously, she blamed Love. Now she is blaming a book: a book about the love of Sir Lancelot for Queen Guinevere. But what kind of love was that? It was an adulterous love. Queen Guinevere was married to King Arthur, and Sir Lancelot had taken an oath to be loyal to the King. And what happened as a result of that adulterous love affair? War broke out, King Arthur was mortally wounded, and Camelot fell as a center of civilization with the result that England fell back into the Dark Ages.

That book was your Galehot, you say. Galehot was the go-between for Lancelot and Guinevere; he was no one you should want to know.

Plus, you did not read that book correctly. That book warns against adultery. Nothing good came out of the adulterous love affair of Sir Lancelot and Queen Guinevere. If you had read that book as the moral warning it is, instead of as the pornography you took it to be, you would not have committed adultery and you would not now be here.

You say, "We closed the book, and that day we read no more." Limbo has a library, and I have read a sentence much like that before in the Confessions *of Saint Augustine. Paolo's name means Paul, and Saint Augustine was converted to Christianity by reading the work of Saint Paul. Like Francesca and Paolo, Augustine read a book. Augustine's book was by Saint Paul, who told him to turn to Christ. Augustine did that. Augustine wrote, "No further would I read; nor needed I." Instead of reading further, Augustine converted to Christianity. Augustine's reading led him to turn to God, but Francesca and Paolo's reading turned them away from God.*

Hearing Francesca's final words, Dante fainted out of pity for her and Paolo.

Dante, Virgil thought, *you are still naïve, and you have allowed yourself to be scammed. God does not make mistakes. Francesca and Paolo are here because they deserve to be here. Exactly the same thing is true of every other sinner in the Inferno. Other sinners will try to scam you, and I hope that you wise up soon.*

You are supposed to learn from these encounters, Dante. You are supposed to learn to take responsibility for your actions and not blame other people and things.

You are supposed to learn that you have reason to help you decide what is right and what is wrong. You are supposed to learn that you have free will, which you can use to choose to do what is right and to avoid doing what is wrong. If you are going to stay out of the Inferno, these are some of the things you must learn. I can't learn them for you.

Chapter 6: The Gluttonous

When Dante regained consciousness, he discovered that he was in a new section of Hell — the third Circle. Here cold rain and hail and snow fell incessantly, creating mud and a stink like that of a gigantic garbage dump.

Dante and Virgil saw Cerberus, a three-headed dog with a swollen belly whose job was to howl incessantly to make the sinners here wish they were deaf, although the sinners also howled. Cerberus is also the guard of the third Circle. Like the sinners, Cerberus was a glutton, and Cerberus often bit the gluttons.

Once again we see a Circle that is devoted to punishing sinners who are guilty of incontinence, Virgil thought. *These sinners were not able to control themselves. They put their desires ahead of their reason. They made their desires — not their reason — supreme in their lives. These sinners ate or drank way too much. They became obese or alcoholic.*

Virgil had been this way before, and he knew what to do. To keep Cerberus busy long enough that he and Dante could pass, Virgil threw heaps of mud down Cerberus' three throats. Busy swallowing the mud, Cerberus let them pass.

The sinners whom Dante and Virgil passed lay on the ground. They seemed to have human form, but they lacked bodies. Only on Judgment Day would their souls be reunited with their bodies.

One sinner saw Dante and quickly sat up and said, "Do you know who I am? We lived at the same time for a while."

Dante looked closely at the sinner, but he admitted, "Your punishment must have changed you because I don't recognize you. But please tell who you are."

The sinner said, "Your own city — Florence, which is filled with envious people — once claimed me as a citizen. I am damned to this Circle because of my sin of gluttony. The Florentines gave me a nickname: Ciacco."

Ciacco is a fitting name for a glutton such as you, Virgil thought. *It means Hog or Pig.*

"Ciacco," Dante said, "I pity you, and I want to cry, but since you mentioned Florence, can you tell me what will happen to that city that I love?

The city has two political parties that fight each other. What is going to happen to them? Are all the men in Florence envious?"

"After much more fighting, one party will drive out the other party," Ciacco replied. "Then within three years the positions will be reversed, and the party that was victorious will be defeated, and the party that was defeated will be victorious. Two men in Florence are just, but no one will listen to them."

I understand more than you do, Dante, Virgil thought. Ciacco is making a prophecy of your upcoming exile when you will be forbidden ever to return to your beloved Florence on pain of death. Like the other souls in the Inferno, I am able to see the future. However, I won't tell you about your upcoming exile. I am your teacher, but teachers don't tell all they know. Some things are better for a student to think about and discover for him- or herself.

Dante asked, "Can you give me some more information, please? What has happened to Farinata degli Uberti, to Tegghiaio Aldobrandini, to Jacopo Rusticucci, and to Mosca dei Lamberti? Where are they? Are they in Heaven or in Hell?"

"They are in Hell," Ciacco answered. "Their sins are worse than mine, so they are in deeper Circles than I am. If you continue your journey downward, you will see them. But if you ever make it again to the sweet, living world, remember me and ask our mutual friends to remember me."

The deeper we go into Hell, the worse the sins that are being punished, Virgil thought. High in Hell, many of the sinners still want to be remembered on Earth. Very low in Hell, many of the sinners prefer to be entirely forgotten on Earth because of the vileness of their sins.

Ciacco's gaze lost focus. He squinted, and then he lay down again in the mud with the other gluttons.

Virgil told Dante, "Ciacco will stay like that until Judgment Day. On that day, his soul will be reunited with his body."

"What will happen when his soul is reunited with his body?" Dante asked. "Will his torment be increased or lessened or just the same as now?"

"You have studied philosophy," Virgil replied. "Human beings were created with both a body and a soul. Together, body and soul are more perfect than they are separately. What is perfect can feel more perfectly than what is not perfect can feel. The sinners in Hell will feel their pain more intently, and the saved souls in the Supreme Emperor's kingdom will feel their bliss more intently."

They continued walking.

This is another example of contrapasso, *Virgil thought. Mud is plentiful in the third Circle of the Inferno because rain is always falling. The gluttons wanted to enjoy the good things, but now they are forced to live in uncomfortable surroundings — surroundings much like a muddy pigsty. The gluttons made pigs of themselves while living, and now, although they are dead, they live like pigs. The gluttons sleep in the mud like pigs, just like a glutton would go to sleep after enjoying a huge meal. After talking with Dante, Ciacco was unable to focus his eyes; he is now in a stupor, just as a glutton would be in a stupor after eating a huge meal. In addition, Cerberus bites the gluttons the way that the gluttons bit into their food.*

Dante and Virgil then saw Plutus, the arch-enemy of Humankind.

Chapter 7: The Wasters, Hoarders, Wrathful, and Sullen

As Virgil and Dante approached him, Plutus clucked the nonsense words "*Papa Satan, pape Satan aleppe!*"

Virgil reassured Dante, "Plutus has no power to stop you from continuing your journey. Therefore, do not be afraid."

Virgil then turned on the wolf-like Plutus and shouted, "Be quiet! This man here is on a mission from the Supreme Emperor!"

Plutus, deflated like a sail in a calm, sank to the ground, and was quiet.

Plutus is an appropriate guard for Circle 4, Virgil thought. *Plutus is also known as Pluto, and he is the pagan god of wealth, as well as the god who ruled the Underworld. It is fitting that he rules the Underworld because much wealth (gold, silver, diamonds) comes from under the ground. His association with wealth makes him a fitting guard for the sinners in Circle 4: the wasters and the hoarders.*

Virgil and Dante saw many souls now — more than in the Circles they had already passed through. These souls pushed heavy weights before them in the Circle, and when they met, they crashed the heavy weights together. One group shouted, "Why hoard?" The other group shouted, "Why waste?" Then they went around the Circle again, and they crashed their heavy weights together again, and they shouted again.

"Who are these sinners?" Dante asked Virgil. "From their haircuts, I see that many of them were priests. Were they all priests on this side?"

"These sinners were incontinent when it came to wealth," Virgil replied. "Neither group could control themselves. One group hoarded their wealth, while the other group wasted their wealth. Many of the sinners you see here were Popes, cardinals, and priests — such people are unfortunately prone to greediness."

Here we see two groups of sinners being punished together because their sins, although opposites, are closely related, Virgil thought. *The wasters and the hoarders are people who either saved as much money as possible and never spent it or people who spent every penny they could and never saved anything. Both types of people are sinners. To be good with money, living people need to spend some money to acquire necessities and good things; however, they also need to have an emergency fund. When it comes to money, living people need to seek a mean between extremes.*

Limbo has a library, and so I am familiar with the work of Aristotle, whom I also studied while I was alive and who is also in Limbo so that I can consult him. The theory of the mean between extremes is a famous part of Aristotle's ethical thought. He believed in moderation — as most Greeks did. If you had too much or too little of something, you would suffer from an excess or a deficiency of that thing. Think about food. If you eat too much food, you will be overweight. If you eat too little food, you will be underweight. You need to eat the right amount of food so that you will have a healthy weight. What you need is exactly the right amount. A different example: Courage is the mean between the extremes of cowardice (deficiency) and rashness (excess). The sinners here failed to find the mean between the extremes of miserliness and of wastefulness.

"Shouldn't I be able to recognize some of the sinners here?" Dante asked Virgil.

"No, you won't be able to recognize anybody here," Virgil replied. "Because of their sinful relationship with wealth, these sinners failed to accomplish anything notable while they were alive. They failed to accomplish something great for Humankind. Because of that, they have no distinguishing characteristics here.

"Well, they do have some distinguishing characteristics, Those who are misers have tight fists; those who are wasters are without hair because they have spent even the hair on their heads. But as for recognizing a sinner and knowing his or her name, forget it.

"These sinners are exactly where they belong. They overvalued either wealth or what wealth can buy, and now no amount of wealth can rescue them from Hell. In Hell as in the living world, they bicker over what belongs to Fortune."

"Who or what is this Fortune that you mention?" Dante asked.

"Fortune controls all the wealth that ever was and ever will be," Virgil replied. "Fortune is a minister of God. She sees that money goes from person to person, family to family, country to country. She controls the Wheel of Fortune. At times, a person may be at the top of the Wheel of Fortune and be very prosperous, but as the Wheel turns, that person's prosperity decreases. The thing to do is to know that the Wheel of Fortune will turn. While riding high on the Wheel of Fortune, save some wealth so that you are at least somewhat prepared when you are riding low on the Wheel of Fortune. The same applies to families and to countries. The Wheel of Fortune turns for individuals, for families as a whole, and for entire countries.

"Human beings dislike Fortune, but they should recognize that she is doing the work of the Supreme Emperor.

"But now let us continue on our journey."

Virgil and Dante continued walking. They came to a spring, which created a stream of grey water, and they walked along the stream on a rough path. As they walked, the stream of grey water turned into a marsh that Dante learned is named the Styx.

In the marsh they saw muddy, angry sinners moving around and fighting each other. Not only did they hit each other with their hands, but they also kicked and bit each other — so great was their anger.

Virgil said, "Here in this Circle — Circle 5 — you see those who could not control their anger. We see the sinners on top of the marsh, yet other sinners are below the marsh, revealing their presence only by the bubbles rising to the top of the marsh.

"These sinners below the marsh say, if you listen closely, 'We were sluggish while we were alive, and in our heart was the smoke of sloth. Now we are punished in the muck of Styx.' So they say, but not clearly."

The sinners below the marsh are the slothful, Virgil thought. The slothful should have pursued the right things while they were alive, but they were slothful — lazy — and did not pursue them with the zeal that they ought to have shown for the right things. Along with their sloth, they were sullen — they bottled up their anger. It would have been better for them if they had expressed vigorous and righteous anger at sin and sinners.

Virgil and Dante continued walking along the path by the marsh. Eventually, they reached a high tower.

Chapter 8: The Boatman Phlegyas and Filippo Argenti

Before Dante and Virgil reached the foot of the high tower, they saw some lights. Two small lights appeared at the top of the tower, and then another light appeared far in the distance. They seemed to be signal lights. The presence of Dante and Virgil had been noticed, and someone or something had been alerted.

Dante asked Virgil, "What is happening here? What do the signal lights mean?"

Virgil replied, "The one who has been summoned is already approaching us across the swamp of the Styx. You should be able to see him approaching us now."

Dante looked and saw a boat crossing the swamp. Only one being was on the boat, and he shouted at Dante and Virgil, "You belong to me, now."

"Phlegyas, you are wrong," Virgil replied. "You will have our company only as long as it takes you to ferry us across the swamp."

Phlegyas was angry. He had thought that Dante was a new soul who would be tormented in the lower Circles of Hell, but he was mistaken.

You are still angry, Phlegyas, Virgil thought. *You have been angry for a long time. You became angry when the god Apollo raped your daughter. You were so angry that you set fire to Apollo's temple at Delphi. Because of that, Apollo killed you. You are a fitting guardian for Circle 5 of Hell, the Circle that punishes the wrathful.*

Phlegyas may have been angry at Dante and Virgil, but nevertheless he knew that he had to ferry them across the Styx. Virgil boarded the boat first. Because souls have no weight, the boat did not sink lower into the water. Dante then boarded the boat, which sank lower into the water, revealing that a living human being was on board.

As the boat crossed the Styx, a sinner in the water saw how heavily loaded the boat was. Knowing that a living human being was on board, and curious, and perhaps wanting to do violence to a living human being, the muddy sinner rose out of the muddy water bond asked, "Who are you, still-living human? Why do you come here before you are dead?"

Dante replied, "I may have come here, but I will not stay here. Who are you, ugly and muddy sinner?"

The sinner replied. "I am one who cries."

"I recognize you," Dante said. "And may you cry and mourn here forever, damn you."

The muddy sinner reached toward the boat, but the ever-vigilant Virgil, Dante's guardian, shoved the soul away from the boat, shouting, "Stay away! Stay with the other sinners!"

Virgil then hugged Dante and said, "You have acted rightly. Blessed are you and the womb that bore you. This sinner was arrogant and no good memories of him exist in the living world. And here he is angry forever. Many living men are like this sinner. They think that they are VIPs in the living world, but after they die they will wallow in the mud of the Styx like pigs in a pigsty."

Yes, you have acted correctly, Virgil thought. *Previously, you felt pity for the sinners. You pitied Francesca da Rimini, charming bitch that she was. You also pitied Ciacco. None of these sinners deserves any pity whatsoever. All of them are exactly where they deserve to be. God does not make mistakes. You are learning, Dante. You are at least beginning to feel righteous indignation, which is the mean between the extremes of irrational anger and sullenness. Sullenness, of course, is bottled-up anger.*

Dante said to Virgil, "I would like to see this sinner punished even more."

"You will see just that," Virgil replied. "A wish such as that deserves to be fulfilled."

Almost immediately, a group of sinners saw the sinner whom Dante hated. They shouted, "Get Filippo Argenti," and they mangled him, making Dante happy.

Dante then began to hear the noise of wailing, and he looked at the tower, which was growing nearer.

"The tower is part of the city of Dis — the city of Lucifer," Virgil said. "Its walls are high, and its residents are fierce."

"I can see part of the city now," Dante said. "I see mosques burning with flames."

"The burning of the mosques provides a reddish light for the lower Circles of Hell," Virgil said.

The boat arrived at the city of Dis. Wanting to get rid of his passengers quickly, Phlegyas shouted, "Get out of my boat now! This is the entrance you seek!"

Dante and Virgil disembarked, and they saw more than a thousand fallen angels — those who had rebelled with Lucifer against God — on the walls of the city. The fallen angels realized that Dante was still alive, and they shouted at him, "Who are you? What living person dares to come into the Land of the Dead? You, dead soul, may approach the city, but the living being may not. You, dead soul, will stay here with us — we will force you to. Let the living being try to retrace, alone, his steps to the living world — if he dares!"

Hearing this, Dante felt great fear. Virgil had been his guide and guardian throughout the Land of the Dead. He did not want to go anywhere in the Inferno without him. He cried to Virgil, "Please don't leave me. You have been my protector, and I need you. If we cannot go forward, let us retrace our steps together."

Virgil replied, "Fear not. No one can prevent us from continuing our journey. Think of the Supreme Emperor and the three Heavenly ladies who want us to take this journey. I will talk to the fallen angels alone. Stay here. Don't worry — I won't leave you alone in the Land of the Dead."

Dante stayed where he was, and Virgil walked off. He did not go out of Dante's sight, but Dante was unable to hear what Virgil and the fallen angels said to each other. Then the fallen angels raced back to the city of Dis.

Virgil was upset when he returned to Dante. Virgil's eyes were downcast, and he murmured, "Who are such beings to forbid me to visit the lower Circles of Hell?"

Then Virgil said to Dante, "Don't worry. This is a minor, temporary setback. These fallen angels cannot keep us from our journey. These fallen angels cause trouble, although they are always conquered. Once they tried to bar the gate into Hell to keep the Mighty Warrior from breaking into Hell and carrying away from Limbo the souls who belong in Paradise. The Mighty Warrior defeated the angels, and now the gate into Hell is always open, forever and forever. Earlier, you saw the words that were written above that gate.

"Already, Heavenly help is on its way. I understand much that concerns reason, but I cannot do everything. This time I need help from Heaven, and that help is already on its way. The Heavenly help will open the gate of Dis so that we may continue on our journey."

Chapter 9: The City of Dis

Dante's face had paled with fear as he saw that Virgil was returning after his unsuccessful attempt to convince the fallen angels to allow them to pass through the gates of the city of Dis.

Virgil waited, looking worried and saying, "We must pass through the gates. Nothing can prevent us from doing that. After all, we have been promised help. Or — no, we will receive help, but it is taking more time than I like for help to get to us."

Dante was afraid, and he asked Virgil, "Has anyone ever traveled to the bottom of the Inferno from Limbo?"

"That is an unusual journey to take," Virgil replied, "but I have traveled it before. Not long after I died, the sorceress Erichtho summoned my spirit to her and gave me a task to travel to the pit of Judas at the bottom of the Inferno and bring out a spirit for her to consult. This is something she had done before. While I was still alive, she sent a soul to the bottom of the Inferno to retrieve another soul who would foretell the victor of the Battle of Pharsalia, in which the forces of Julius Caesar defeated the forces of Pompey. Because I have traveled throughout the Inferno, I well know the path that we will take and I am familiar with the place we are now. This swamp of the Styx completely surrounds the city of Dis, which we *will* enter although not — as you know — without some trouble."

As they talked, Dante looked up at the city, and above its walls he suddenly saw the three Furies — the Erinyes — fly. They were winged avenging spirits covered with blood — they had snakes for hair, and their purpose in the ancient world was to wreck vengeance against children who killed their parents. These were the avenging spirits who pursued Orestes after he killed his mother, who had killed his father.

Virgil looked up, and he saw the Furies, whom he recognized: "Look! Megaera is on the left, Alecto on the right, and Tisiphone in the middle!" Virgil knew much about the Furies. Alecto had maddened Queen Amata and Turnus to rebel against and fight Aeneas when he and his refugee Trojans tried to establish themselves in Italy. Virgil knew how dangerous the Furies could be.

The Furies hovered in the air, shrieking and tearing their skin with their fingernails, drawing blood. They shouted, "Come, Medusa, and turn this living man into stone. We let Theseus get away from us too easily."

This is a threat that needs to be taken seriously, Virgil thought. *Any living human being who looks at Medusa, who also has snakes for hair, will instantly be turned into stone. In addition, the Furies and Medusa are still angry because Hercules released Theseus from the Inferno when he came into the Inferno to take Cerberus the three-headed dog to the Land of the Living.*

Virgil told Dante, "Turn around and cover your eyes because if you see Medusa your journey is over and you will not return to the Land of the Living."

Dante did as he was told, and Virgil also covered Dante's eyes with his hands. In doing so, both Dante and Virgil underestimated the power of God and of God's helpers.

Now came an important event. Sound blasted through the Inferno, and Hell trembled. A hurricane will tear through a forest, uprooting trees and destroying everything in its path. Such seemed to be this sound.

Virgil removed his hands from over Dante's eyes and told him, "Turn around and look."

Dante saw over a thousand sinners diving into the muddy marsh of the Styx the way that frogs will dive into the water to get away from snakes, their natural enemies. Then he saw a good angel walking on the water of the Styx, which did not even wet his feet. The good angel did not fear; instead, the good angel was filled with scorn for the sinners and the fallen angels.

Dante was going to speak to Virgil, but Virgil motioned for him to keep silent and to bow low.

The good angel reached the gate of Dis and touched it with his wand, and the gate immediately opened.

Filled with scorn, the good angel said to the fallen angels, "What do you think you are doing? You know that you are powerless against the One Who sent me. You gain nothing but defeat by opposing Him. As you should have learned by now, Ultimate Evil is powerless against Ultimate Good. When Lucifer rebelled against God, you fought on the side of Lucifer. Look where it got you!"

This is much like another opening of a gate of Hell, Virgil thought. *When the Mighty Warrior came to rescue the righteous saved souls from Limbo, these fallen angels opposed him, but nevertheless he rescued the souls, causing pain to those sinners who were and are condemned to reside in the Inferno forever. He also caused pain to the fallen angels who opposed Him just as this angel from the Supreme Emperor is causing pain to those fallen angels once again.*

The angel from God left; his face showed that he was thinking of more important things than opening the gate — something that was a mere distraction for him.

Dante and Virgil approached the gate of Dis and passed through it. No fallen angel dared oppose them.

Past the gate, Dante saw an ugly landscape. It was filled with sepulchers. These burial chambers were not closed; from them flames leapt up. From the inside of the burial chambers came cries of grief and pain.

Dante asked Virgil, "What kind of sinners are these who reside in the open tombs?"

"Arch-heretics and their disciples are buried here," Virgil replied. "The tombs hold many more sinners than you suspect, and each kind of heretic is entombed with the other heretics who believed incorrectly about God. The tombs burn more brightly for the greater heresies."

Dante and Virgil walked toward the tombs.

I can understand why the guards here are the fallen angels and the Furies and Medusa, Dante thought. Medusa and the Furies are appropriate guards of this Circle because they are pagan figures, and of course pagans do not think correctly about God. The fallen angels are also appropriate guards of this Circle that is devoted to punishing heretics because they did not think correctly about God, as they chose to fight against Him rather than fight against Lucifer. Heresy is thinking incorrectly about God; the fallen angels, the Furies, and Medusa thought incorrectly about God. Still, tombs don't need guards, so the guards here need hardly keep a close eye on the sinners in the tombs.

Chapter 10: Heretics in Flaming Tombs

As Dante and Virgil walked among the flaming tombs, Dante asked, "Can the people in these tombs be seen? After all, the lids are off the tombs. And the guards are not here, but on the tower and the walls of the City of Dis."

Virgil replied, "Right now, the tombs are open, but on Judgment Day these sinful souls will be reunited with their sinful bodies, and then the tombs will be closed forever. Here you see the part of the cemetery where Epicurus and his followers lie. They committed heresy by not believing in life after death."

This is another example of contrapasso, Virgil thought. *These heretical sinners did not believe in life after death. They believed instead that when they died they would be in a tomb forever, and that is exactly what will happen to them.*

"You ask: Can you speak to these souls?" Virgil continued. "That question will be answered for you very quickly. So will the question that you want to ask me but you have not asked yet."

"I have not yet asked it because I am afraid of talking too much," Dante said.

Just then, a figure stood up in the tomb, which was sunken into the ground. The top of his body was visible. The sinner said, "Oh, Tuscan, because of your accent I know that you are from Florence, my own city — a city on which I was perhaps too harsh while I was alive. Talk to me."

Dante, startled, drew closer to Virgil, who said, "Turn around and look at Farinata degli Uberti, who while he was alive was a big man in your part of the world."

Dante turned around and looked at Farinata, who stood like a statue. His face showed his disdain for the Hell he was in.

Virgil gently pushed Dante toward Farinata, the better for Dante to speak to the sinner, but Virgil also advised Dante, "Be careful which words you speak."

Yes, Farinata, Virgil thought. *You are standing like the statue that you wish the Florentines would raise to you. You are proud, and you wish to be impressive as you stand here. But half of your body is in the tomb and half of your body is sticking out of the tomb. Although you would like to tower over Dante, Dante stands higher than you do. Although you would like to look like a dignified statue on a pedestal, you look somewhat silly.*

When Dante was standing alongside the tomb in which Farinata stood, the sinner said to him with contempt, "And just who are *your* ancestors?"

Dante told him. Because Dante was very familiar with Farinata's biography, which was important in the history of Florence, he knew that Farinata's family was very high born and much classier than Dante's own family.

Farinata listened as Dante explained who his family was, and then Farinata said, "Your family was a bitter enemy of mine and to my family and my political party. I fought against them and scattered them not just once but twice."

This is at least partly true, Dante thought. *Farinata and his family were Ghibellines, while my family consists of Guelfs. The Ghibellines exiled the Guelfs from Florence twice: in 1248 and in 1260. However, my party, the Guelfs, came back from exile twice and as we speak they are in fact still in control of Florence.*

A little angry, Dante said to Farinata, "You expelled them from Florence not just once but twice, but they returned to Florence not just once but twice. Returning from exile is an art that your family has not mastered."

Just then, another shade popped his head above the tomb that Farinata was standing in. This sinner looked around as if he expected to see someone. That someone was not present, and the sinner began to cry. The sinner then said to Dante, "If your great genius as a poet makes it possible for you to visit the Inferno although you are still alive, then why isn't my son here with you?"

Dante recognized the sinner. He was Cavalcante de' Cavalcanti, a Guelf. Farinata was a Ghibelline, so they were of opposing political parties. However, they were related by marriage — Cavalcante's son had married Farinata's daughter in a politically motivated marriage. This son was named Guido, and he was a poet whom Cavalcante considered to be at least the equal of Dante.

Dante replied, "Your son is not with me, but I am not alone. My guide is a poet whom Guido, your son, did not respect."

Be careful here, Virgil thought. *I see a lot of pride. Farinata is obviously proud, standing as he does in imitation of the statue he wishes the Florentines would erect to him. Cavalcante is obviously proud of his son — overly proud, in fact, since you, Dante, are much the better poet. But Dante, do you really think that your great poetic genius is the reason why you are here in the Inferno? That is not the reason. You are here because you messed up your life so badly that three Heavenly ladies are going out of their way to teach you the right way to live your life so that you may avoid being damned when you die. This trip through the Inferno is not a reward for your great genius — although you are in fact a great poet. Instead, this is a last-ditch effort to keep you from being damned to Hell when you die.*

Cavalcante jumped up in the tomb and said, "You say that he *did* not respect your guide? Do you mean that my son is dead?"

Dante was surprised. The sinners were aware of the past, and he had heard them prophesy, so they knew the future. Why wouldn't the sinners also know what was happening in the present? Because of his shock, he did not answer Cavalcante quickly, and the sinner disappeared back down in the tomb.

Farinata completely ignored Cavalcante. Instead, he started talking to Dante as if they had not been interrupted: "If they did not master the art of returning from exile, that causes me more pain than my damnation. But you yourself will learn within 50 months how hard such an art is to master. But tell me, why is your political party so hard on my family? Why won't your political party allow my family to return to Florence?"

"Your question is easy to answer," Dante replied. "It is because of the blood that stained the Arbia River red."

Yes, Dante thought, *we Florentines remember that battle well. The Arbia River flows by the hill named Montaperti. In 1260, five years before I was born, you and the Ghibellines, including Ghibellines you had recruited from Siena, fought the Battle of Montaperti. You Ghibellines defeated the Guelfs and stained the Arbia River red with Guelf blood. But the Guelfs later regained control of Florence. In 1280, many Ghibellines were allowed to return to Florence; however, your family — the Uberti family — was not allowed to return to Florence. Why not? Because you got so many Florentines killed.*

Farinata sighed and said, "I was not the only one fighting in the battle. But after the battle, when everyone else was thinking of destroying Florence, I was the only one who opposed the city's destruction."

Yes, you did, Virgil thought, *but why did you do that? You fought against the Guelfs because you wanted political power in Florence. If Florence were totally destroyed, you would not be able to have power there. Like the other sinners in the Inferno, you are self-serving. You don't want to take full responsibility for the blood shed in the Battle of Montaperti, and you do want to take full credit for saving the city of Florence when actually you wanted to save Florence just so you could rule it.*

"Can you answer a question for me?" Dante asked. "I have been wondering for a while and have refrained from asking my guide how it is that you and the others here know the future but do not seem to have knowledge of the present."

"We in Hell have faulty vision," Farinata replied. "We do see the future, but we do not know what is happening in the Land of the Living at the present time. Only when a new sinner arrives here do we get news of present events in the Land of the Living. When Judgment Day comes and the tombs are closed forever, we will have no knowledge at all."

This is true, Virgil thought. *After Judgment Day, no future events will occur. Every soul will be in its proper place, enjoying bliss eternally or suffering torment eternally.*

Dante then requested, "Will you tell Cavalcanti that his son is still alive? I did not answer him earlier because I was surprised that sinners here could have knowledge of the future and yet not have knowledge of the present."

Dante, you are still naïve, Virgil thought. *Do you think that Farinata will ever acknowledge the existence of Cavalcante, even though Cavalcante's son married his daughter? They will be tombmates forever, and they will not acknowledge each other's existence forever. Farinata is not going to deliver your message.*

Also, note that Cavalcante misunderstood you. He thought that you were saying that his son is dead, but you were not saying that. Heretics misunderstand God and religion.

Also, note that the sinners in the Inferno have faulty vision. They certainly had faulty vision when it came to the Supreme Emperor.

Finally, note the interruptions that we have seen here. Farinata interrupted you and me as we were talking, and Cavalcante interrupted you and Farinata as you two were talking. Obviously, we have people not communicating well here. People who oppose each other do not communicate well with each other — and sometimes they do not communicate at all.

Virgil then called to Dante to come — they must continue their journey. Still, Dante asked one more question of Farinata: "With whom do you share your tomb?"

Farinata replied, "More than a thousand souls are here, including Emperor Frederick II and Cardinal Ottaviano degli Ubaldini. The others I shall not mention."

You are still proud, even in Hell, Virgil thought. *You mention the names of two VIPs, but not the names of your other tombmates. Pride is a deadly sin, and look where it got you.*

Dante looked troubled as he remembered what Farinata had said about him — "you yourself will learn within 50 months how hard such an art is to master" — and Virgil said to him, "You have heard a prophecy of your future life. Remember it. Later, you will meet one who will clearly explain your future to you."

The two continued their journey.

Dante, I don't think that you learned what you should have learned here, Virgil thought. *Whenever you speak to a sinner, you have something that you should learn. Here you talked to two sinners who are guilty of heresy. You are not a heretic, and so you did not speak specifically about heresy here, but about something that is related to heresy: factionalism — specifically factionalism in politics and in poetry. Factionalism, or parties battling each other, can be seen in politics, in religion, and even in art, including poetry. Obviously, factionalism exists in politics, as we see with the Ghibellines and the Guelfs, and with the White Guelfs and the Black Guelfs. Extreme factionalism can be very bad, indeed. When a new faction comes into power in Florence, it bans the opposing faction, exiling them from Florence. Although factionalism can be seen in politics, as in the struggle between the Ghibellines and the Guelfs, or between the White Guelfs and the Black Guelfs, we also see factionalism in other areas. For example, we can see factionalism in religion, as when we see the heretics being combated by those who have the true beliefs concerning religion and God. Factionalism can also exist in poetry. A new kind of poetry can replace the old style of poetry. A modern poet can disrespect an ancient poet.*

Dante, what you should have learned here is to avoid extreme factionalism. I hope that you will learn that lesson as we continue our journey. I don't think you have learned that lesson yet. Instead, you and Farinata were battling each other verbally. Farinata pointed out that he had exiled your political party twice, then you pointed out that your political party had returned from exile twice but that his family had not returned from exile, and then Farinata prophesied that you would be sent into exile. Instead of your learning to avoid extreme factionalism, you and Farinata were engaging in it. Instead of talking together as citizens of the same city, you and Farinata were battling each other verbally. Farinata engaged in extreme factionalism during his life, and he ended up in the Inferno. Dante, unless you learn to avoid extreme factionalism, you may end up in the Inferno.

35

Chapter 11: Virgil Teaches Dante

Dante and Virgil arrived at a steep bank from which they could look down into the dark, deep pit of Hell. They did not stay there long, for the stench arising from the lower Circles was too rank for them to bear. They moved back from the edge of the pit onto a tomb. On the tomb was written a name and a sin. The name was that of Pope Anastasius II, and his sin was to be a heretical follower of Photinus, who denied the divinity of Christ, believing instead that both of His parents were mortal human beings.

Virgil said to Dante, "We cannot continue on our journey yet. We will stay here a while so that we can become accustomed to the stench arising from the lower Circles of Hell. Once we have become used to the stench, we will continue our journey."

Dante replied, "That's fine, but I don't want to waste time while we wait. Do you have any ideas?"

Well done, Virgil thought. *You don't want to waste time, and indeed time is not a thing to be wasted, especially now, when you are on a journey to save your soul.*

"Yes," Virgil replied. "As we wait here, I will be able to tell you how Hell is organized. That way, you will be better prepared for what is to come.

"First, let's have a review. Even before entering Hell Proper, you saw the Vestibule of Hell, where those who did not choose between good and evil are punished. These souls are not worthy of Heaven, and Hell does not want them. These souls did nothing memorable — good or bad — with their lives.

"After passing through the gate above which are words written by God, we crossed the River Acheron and you saw my residence in Limbo, the first Circle of Hell. In that place the virtuous pagans and the unbaptized reside. It is a place of sighs, not screams.

"Then you saw the first of the three great divisions of Hell according to the pagan idea of sin: incontinence, violence, and fraud. The sins of incontinence are less evil than the sins of violence and of fraud because the sins of incontinence are those of a lack of self-control, not of malice aforethought.

"Circles 2 through 5 are devoted to the sins of incontinence. In Circle 2 are punished those who could not control their lust. In Circle 3 are punished those who could not control their desire for food and drink. In Circle 4 are punished the prodigal and the miserly: those who could not control their desire either for money or for the things that money can buy. In Circle 5 are punished those who could not control their anger.

"In Circle 6 are those who committed heresy. Because heresy is an essentially Christian sin, it is outside the pagan classification of sins.

"Below are the final three Circles of Hell. These Circles are devoted to punishing those who are guilty of malice, which is committed through violence or fraud. Fraud is something that is committed only by human beings — animals are violent but do not commit fraud — and so God hates fraud more than he hates violence.

"In Circle 7 are punished those who have committed violence. There are three kinds of violence:

"One, a sinner can be violent against neighbors. A sinner can do this by harming the person or by harming the person's property.

"Two, a sinner can be violent against self by committing suicide. A sinner can also be violent against self by so violently wasting his wealth that he courts death.

"Three, a sinner can be violent against God by blaspheming Him. A sinner can also be violent against God by opposing Nature, which God created; for example, the Sodomites oppose Nature by engaging in sex that is incapable of resulting in children.

"In Circles 8 and 9 are punished those who are guilty of committing fraud. Fraud is depriving another person of a right through the use of willful misrepresentation.

"The two major kinds of fraud are simple and complex. Simple fraud is punished in Circle 8. Simple fraud does not involve the betrayal of a special trust.

"Ten kinds of sinners engage in simple fraud:
"One, Seducers and Panders,
"Two, Flatterers,
"Three, Simonists,
"Four, Fortune-Tellers and Sorcerers,
"Five, Grafters — those who give or accept bribes,
"Six, Hypocrites,

"Seven, Thieves,

"Eight, Evil Deceivers/Those Who Misuse Great Gifts,

"Nine, Schismatics; that is, those who caused divisions (in families, in politics, in religion, etc.), and

"Ten, Falsifiers; that is, Alchemists, Evil Impersonators, Counterfeiters, and Liars.

"Complex fraud is punished in Circle 9. Complex fraud does involve the betrayal of a special trust. Complex fraud is fraud to which is added treachery toward those to whom we have a special obligation to be honest and forthright. Four kinds of sinners engage in complex fraud:

"One, Traitors against kin/family,

"Two, Traitors against government,

"Three, Traitors against guests or hosts, and

"Four, Traitors against God — the worst sin possible."

Dante said to Virgil, "I don't understand why the sinners in Circle 5, those who could not control their anger, are not punished in Circle 7 along with those who are violent. We saw the sinners in Circle 5 fighting each other. Isn't that violence?"

"The two sins are different," Virgil replied. "In Circle 5 are punished those who are guilty of one kind of intemperance — they did not control their anger. The violence they do is not out of malice but rather out of intemperance.

"In Circle 7 (and Circles 8 and 9) are punished those who are guilty of malice. Instead of being guilty of not controlling themselves, they are guilty of using their self-control to deliberately commit violence (or fraud)."

"I have one more question," Dante said. "How is usury offensive to God?"

Virgil replied, "Human industry and Nature are related. Human beings are meant to work the way that Nature does. A farmer does good by growing plants. This is the sort of work that human beings are supposed to do. A craftsman also works with Nature by taking raw materials and turning them into useful products. A usurer lends money at interest and makes money that way. The usurer does not make anything; the usurer produces neither food nor useful items. God wants human beings to work with Nature and to be productive.

"Now we are ready to continue our journey. We have grown used to the stench, and you now have a better understanding of the organization of Hell."

I think you have learned quite a lot, Virgil thought. *You have learned the main point: The deeper you go into Hell, the worst the sins become. The sins of incontinence are the least evil. Lust is the least evil sin of all. The sins of incontinence are punished outside the walls of the city of Dis, which is the city of Lucifer. The sins of heresy, violence, and fraud are punished within the walls of the city of Dis.*

The sins of fraud are the most evil. The sins of complex fraud are more evil than the sins of simple fraud. Being a traitor against God is the worst sin possible. As you would expect, Lucifer, the angel who led the rebellion against God, is the worst sinner of all time.

Chapter 12: The Minotaur and the River of Boiling Blood

As Dante and Virgil continued on their journey, they saw ruins. They also saw the Minotaur, one of the guards of Circle 7.

I know your story, Dante thought about the Minotaur. *You are the half-human, half-bull offspring of Pasiphaë, the wife of King Minos of Crete, who is now the judge of the damned in the Inferno. Virgil and I saw him earlier. Pasiphaë fell in love with a bull, and in order to have sex with the bull, she crept inside a lifelike cow that she ordered the skilled inventor Daedalus to create. The result of their sexual union was the half-bull, half-man Minotaur, which was so violent that Daedalus created a labyrinth for the Minotaur to live in. The Minotaur feasted on the flesh of young Athenians who were given to the Cretans as tribute and put into the labyrinth with him. Eventually, Theseus, the King of Athens, was able to kill the Minotaur. He was afraid that he would get lost in the labyrinth, but Ariadne, Pasiphaë's daughter, helped him by telling him to tie one end of a ball of string to the entrance, then enter the Labyrinth. He was able to find his way out of the Labyrinth by using the string.*

The Minotaur saw Dante and Virgil. The sight so enraged the monster that it began to bite itself.

Virgil called to the Minotaur, "Do you think that you are seeing Theseus again — the man who killed you? You are mistaken, beast! The man who is with me is here to see your misery."

The Minotaur then began to twist and turn with anger, the way that a bull does just before it dies.

Virgil said to Dante, "Run past the Minotaur while it is distracted by its anger."

Virgil and Dante made it past the Minotaur, and they began to climb over the ruins they saw, the result of a great earthquake. As Dante climbed over the ruins, the rocks moved, unaccustomed as they were to the weight of a living man.

"The last time I climbed down here to this Circle, there were no ruins," Virgil said. "I remember that an earthquake struck just before the Mighty Warrior took from Limbo the souls of those who were destined for Heaven.

You know that event as the Harrowing of Hell. That earthquake caused the ruins you see here.

"But now look into the valley. There you will see a river of boiling blood in which are punished those who were physically violent against others."

Dante looked, and in addition to the river of boiling blood he saw Centaurs — beings with the body of a horse but the torso, arms, and head of a man. They were the guards here, and they were armed with bows and arrows.

Have you noticed that so many guards in the Inferno are half-man, half-beast? Virgil thought. *There is a reason for that. Sin can be bestial in nature. Certainly, the sins of violence are bestial in nature; after all, many animals are red in tooth and claw because they kill other animals in order to eat them. Human beings at their finest are not like animals; human beings at their worst are very much like carnivorous animals.*

The Centaurs saw Dante and Virgil, and one shouted at them, "Who are you, and for what Circle of Hell are you destined? Speak, or I will draw my bow!"

Virgil shouted at the Centaur, "I will answer your questions when we reach you and can talk to Chiron. You are as rash as ever, so I won't answer you now."

Virgil then said to Dante, "Not all of the Centaurs are violent — Chiron, the leader of the Centaurs, was the noted tutor of Hercules, the ancient physician Aesculapius, and Achilles — but enough Centaurs are violent that they are appropriate guards of the violent who physically harmed others.

"The Centaur who challenged us is Nessus, who is violent. He seized Hercules' wife, Dejanira, and tried to rape her. Hercules killed Nessus with an arrow that had been dipped in the poisonous blood of the monstrous Hydra, but before Nessus died, he told Dejanira to soak a shirt with his blood, and if she ever doubted Hercules' fidelity to her, to have him wear that shirt. When Dejanira later gave Hercules the shirt to wear, the Hydra-poisoned blood of the Centaur burned Hercules' skin so painfully that he committed suicide.

"Many of the Centaurs are as violent as Nessus. In Thessaly, the Centaurs were invited to a wedding, but grew drunk and tried to rape the women guests.

"As you can see, the Centaurs are the guards here. Being immersed in the river of boiling blood punishes these sinners who were physically violent against other people. These violent people caused the blood of other people to flow; now they are immersed in blood. Each sinner is appointed a certain level to be immersed in the river; the more blood the sinner caused to flow on earth, the more deeply they are immersed in the river. Centaurs shoot arrows at sinners who try to rise above their appointed level in the river."

When Virgil and Dante reached the group of three Centaurs, Chiron, their leader, said to the other Centaurs, "Have you noticed how this one moves the stones he steps on? He is alive! The souls of dead people can't do what he does!"

"This man is indeed alive," Virgil said to Chiron. "My divine duty is to take him through Hell — a journey that he makes out of necessity. A soul from Heaven gave me this task. This living man is not a sinner trying to escape from Hell, and I am acting in accordance with the will of the Heavenly lady who came to me.

"Please give us a guide to escort us across the river of boiling blood at the ford. This living man needs to be carried over."

Chiron ordered Nessus, "You be their guide and escort. Make sure that no one interferes with them."

Obviously, Chiron is intelligent, Virgil thought. *He realized that Dante is a living man, and he immediately made up his mind to help us.*

As they moved along the river of boiling blood, Nessus pointed out some of the sinners being punished. Among the sinners up to their eyelids in boiling blood are cruel tyrants such as Alexander the Great. According to the Christian historian Orosius, Alexander the Great was cruel and violent. Attila the Hun, another noted warrior, is also immersed in boiling blood here. Being immersed in boiling blood up to his eyelids punishes Ezzelino, who burned 11,000 people at the stake on one occasion, here. Other violent sinners are up to their chests, waists, knees, or feet in blood.

As Nessus, Dante, and Virgil moved along the river, it got shallower and shallower until they reached the ford, and Nessus carried Dante and Virgil across it. Dante and Virgil dismounted, and Nessus crossed the river and returned to Chiron.

Dante did not speak to anyone here, nor did he need to, Virgil thought. *Although Dante has sinned, violence is not one of his sins.*

Chapter 13: The Suicides

Not yet had Nessus reached the other bank of the river of boiling blood than Dante and Virgil were walking in a forest that did not have a path. No green leaves could be seen, but only black leaves. No smooth branches could be seen, but only entangled and crooked branches. No fruit could be seen, but only poisonous thorns. No grubby wood such as this exists anywhere in the Land of the Living.

Here were the Harpies, who are half-human and half-bestial. Part of them is female and human, and part of them is a bird. With their human faces, they shriek, and with their wings, they fly.

"Remember where you are," Virgil told Dante. "We have left the river of boiling blood, and soon we will be in a desert of burning sand. Right now, we are in the second of the three areas that punish those sinners who are guilty of violence. This wood is more remarkable than you think right now. Look carefully around you. I will not tell you what you are seeing because you would not believe my words."

Dante looked, and he listened. All he saw were grubby shrubs, but he could hear the sounds of lament coming from somewhere — he knew not where — in addition to the shrieks of the Harpies. Puzzled by the sounds of lament, he stopped.

One of Virgil's powers was being able to read Dante's mind. He knew why Dante was puzzled, and so he said, "Break off one of the branches you see in this forest, and your puzzlement will vanish."

Dante broke off a branch, and the place where the branch had been attached to the shrub oozed with blood. The blood bubbled, and a voice complained, "Why do you injure me by tearing off one of my branches? Why don't you pity the pain I am suffering? All of us shrubs were human beings once, but even if we had been snakes you should show us more pity."

Dante dropped the branch he had broken off.

Virgil said to the sinner whose branch had been broken off, "I knew that my companion would never believe with words alone what he is now seeing, so I urged him to break your branch. Unfortunately, even though I wrote about a similar event in my *Aeneid*, I knew that my companion would not believe unless he had direct experience."

That is true, Virgil thought. *In my* Aeneid, *Aeneas broke a branch and then the shrub began to bleed and to speak to him. It turned out that Polydorus, a Prince of Troy, was buried there. The prince was murdered with spears so the murderers could take his wealth. The body fell to the ground, and the spears took root and grew.*

"Please, tell my companion who you were. He can keep your name alive in the Land of the Living. You need not be forgotten. My companion is still alive, and he will return to the Land of the Living."

"Your words please me very much," the shrub said. "I want to be remembered. My name is Pier delle Vigne — Peter of the Vines. I served the Holy Roman Emperor Frederick II."

Pay attention, Dante, Virgil thought. *Remember who Frederick II is. Frederick II fought the Pope for control of Italy. He died in 1250, and we know that Frederick II ended up in the Inferno in a tomb with Farinata, so we know that he died an unrepentant sinner.*

"I was the Chief of Staff to Frederick II," Pier delle Vigne continued. "I controlled who got access to the Holy Roman Emperor. I also advised Frederick II — I advised him on whether something was good or bad. I served him so faithfully that I lost sleep through overwork as well as losing my life. Envy turned up in the court of Frederick II, who was my Caesar. Envy made all the others my enemies, and my enemies turned Frederick II — my Augustus — against me. False accusations were made about me, and they were believed. Even though I was loyal and just to Frederick II, I behaved unjustly against myself. When you return to the Land of the Living, tell everyone that I was loyal to my emperor. Tell everyone that I am here because of the blow that Envy gave me."

Be careful, Dante, Virgil thought. *Like other sinners in the Inferno, Pier delle Vigne has told his story in a very self-serving way. He is blaming Envy for his problems. Envy turned everyone against him. Envious people convinced Frederick II that Pier was disloyal to him, so he put Pier in prison. While in prison, Pier committed suicide. Of course, we know that Pier — not Envy — was the person who committed suicide. In addition, Pier delle Vigne overvalued Frederick II, whom he calls "Caesar" and "Augustus." And because Pier is in the Inferno, we know that he undervalued God. Of course, although Pier delle Vigne was loyal to Frederick II during Pier's life, he was disloyal to God when he committed suicide.*

Virgil then said to Dante, "If you wish to know anything more, ask your questions now."

"You may ask him questions," Dante replied. "I am so overcome with pity for him that I cannot say anything more to him."

Why are you overcome with pity? Virgil thought. *Do you pity him because of the false accusations that envious people made against him? That kind of pity is acceptable. Or do you pity him because he committed suicide? That kind of pity is unacceptable. I hope that you are learning not to allow yourself to be scammed by these sinners who, after all, are exactly where they ought to be. I hope that you have learned something since you spoke with Francesca da Rimini.*

And, Dante, you have much to learn here. You will be under attack one day. You will lose your political position, and you will be exiled. Like Pier delle Vigne, you will be discouraged and you will wonder whether life is worth living.

The main thing you can learn here is to not act like Pier delle Vigne. Pier delle Vigne committed suicide, and he ended up in the Inferno. If you, Dante, commit suicide when you are discouraged, you can end up in the same place as Pier delle Vigne.

I know that you will be sent into exile, and I know that you will be discouraged, but if you wish to stay away from eternal punishment in the Inferno, you must respond to your discouragement differently from the way that Pier delle Vigne responded to his discouragement.

As human beings, we have free will, and we can choose how we respond to disaster. We can give in to discouragement and commit suicide, or we can respond in a more courageous way.

Virgil then said to Pier delle Vigne, "So that my companion may keep your name, please tell him how souls become shrubs here, and please tell him whether a soul will ever leave these shrubs."

"Briefly," Pier said, "after a person commits suicide, Minos judges his soul and sends it here in Circle 7. The soul drops in this wood the way a seed drops. The soul germinates like a seed and grows into a shrub. The Harpies then feast on it, breaking its branches and causing it pain. By breaking a shrub's branches, the Harpies give it an outlet through which to express grief as the blood comes bubbling from the wound.

"Like the other souls in the Inferno, we will be given our bodies on Judgment Day, but our soul will not be reunited with our body. Instead, our body will hang from our branches. We rejected our body, and therefore it will not be reunited with our soul."

Here we have another contrapasso, *Virgil thought. The suicides are the grubby shrubs of this wood. The suicides cannot even determine when they will talk; they can communicate only when one of their twigs or branches is broken because they use the resulting hole as a mouth until the blood congeals — the blood oozes from the wound the way that sap oozes from a broken twig or branch.*

The punishment of the suicides is appropriate because by killing themselves, the suicides gave up the privilege of self-determination. As shrubs, the suicides have no free will because plants have no free will. This is appropriate because in life the suicides rejected free will by committing suicide.

Because the suicides gave up their privilege of self-determination, they no longer have self-determination in the Inferno. Minos throws their souls into Circle 7, and the souls sprout wherever they fall. As grubby shrubs, the suicides cannot move around, and they cannot even speak unless someone breaks off a twig or branch.

The suicides have no free will because they rejected the chance to use free will to solve their problems. The suicides rejected their bodies, so they will not be reunited with their bodies.

In life, the suicides mutilated themselves. Now, as shrubs, they can no longer mutilate themselves.

Just then, Virgil and Dante heard the sound of a hunt when dogs chase their prey. Two naked souls came running, crashing amidst the shrubs and breaking many branches, causing the souls who were the shrubs to cry out in pain.

One of the naked souls said, "I wish that death would come quickly."

The other naked soul replied, "Lano, you did not run so quickly when you were in battle."

I know who these sinners are, Virgil thought. They are Lano of the wealthy Maconi family and Giacomo da Sant' Andrea. They are Profligates who violently wasted their wealth so they are here in the Circle that punishes the violent. Giacomo da Sant' Andrea once deliberately set on fire several houses that he owned just because he wanted to. Lano of Siena violently wasted his wealth, and then he deliberately sought death in a 1287 battle; he could have escaped by retreating, but stayed to fight so that he would die. That is a kind of suicide.

The spendthrifts who are punished in Circle 4 merely wasted their wealth, while the profligates here in Circle 7 violently wasted their wealth and then courted death.

Tired, Giacomo da Sant' Andrea hid himself among the shrubs, while Lano continued running. The black dogs that had been pursuing the two profligates found Giacomo da Sant' Andrea and tore him to pieces, and then they carried away the pieces in their mouths.

While tearing apart Giacomo da Sant' Andrea, the black dogs also broke many branches of the shrub, and Virgil brought Dante close so that he could hear the shrub complain: "Giacomo da Sant' Andrea, why did you hide in me? You have brought me much pain because you brought to me the black dogs that tore my branches and took my leaves from me."

Virgil asked the shrub, "Who are you?"

The shrub answered, "I am a Florentine who committed suicide by hanging myself in my home. The first patron of Florence was Mars, the Roman god of war. But Florence exchanged this patron for John the Baptist, whose image is stamped on the gold coins of Florence. Because of this, Mars swears that endless sorrow will come to Florence."

Chapter 14: The Desert with Falling Flames

Because of Dante's love of Florence, he gathered up the leaves that had been torn from the bush that was the soul of the anonymous Florentine, and he left them by the bush.

Dante and Virgil continued walking, and they reached the third part of Circle 7. Already they had seen the river of boiling blood and the wood of the suicides. Now they came to a desert of burning sand. Nothing grew here, and nothing could ever grow here. Nothing was in this infertile desert but burning-hot sand and the flakes of fire that rained continuously down on the suffering sinners.

The sinners were of three kinds. Some sinners lay on their backs, facing upward. Other sinners were hunched over looking at something hanging from their necks. Yet other sinners were continuously running.

The greatest number of sinners belonged to the groups who were continuously running, but the loudest sinners were those who lay on their backs because they were most exposed to the falling flakes of flame and so they suffered the most.

The pain felt here came from two places: above and below. The flames fell from above, but the sand below was so hot that it burned all the sinners where they touched it.

Almost everywhere sinners were constantly moving their hands to put out the flames that fell on them. First on one side and then on the other side, flames fell. First on one side and then on the other side, hands moved to put out the flames. The dance of the hands was almost universal. Just one sinner did not deign to put out the flames.

Dante asked Virgil, "Who is the sinner who ignores the flames? Although he could move his hands to put them out, he does not."

The sinner heard Dante and replied for Virgil: "I am the same here in Hell as I was while I was alive. Jupiter killed me because I blasphemed. I was one of the seven who attacked Thebes, and I challenged any of the gods, including Jupiter, to attempt to withstand me. Jupiter heard my boast and my challenge, and he killed me with a thunderbolt."

Virgil then said to the sinner, "Capaneus, yes, you blasphemed against your god, and so you are punished here. Your sullenness and pride make the pain you feel even worse because they stop you from brushing the flames away from your body."

Virgil turned to Dante and said, "As Capaneus has said, he was one of the seven kings who attacked Thebes. His blasphemy has sentenced him here, and here he is still blaspheming."

Virgil thought, *The blasphemers, sodomites, and greedy moneylenders are punished in this scorching desert. All of these sinners have committed sins in which they are violent against God or God's gifts. All of these sinners have committed sins in which they either take something that should be fertile and make it infertile or take something that should be infertile and make it fertile. These sinners are on a sandy, infertile desert on which fire rains down and on which nothing can grow.*

The blasphemers ought to have loved God, but they cursed God instead. The love of God ought to be fertile and result in good things, but the blasphemers cursed something that ought to be regarded as valuable. Now they lie in the burning, infertile desert and face upward, looking toward that which they cursed. Of course, when they open their mouths to curse God, flakes of fire fall into their mouths.

In contrast, the greedy moneylenders took something that ought to be infertile and made it fertile. The Bible, which Dante has studied, is against lending money at interest to relatives or to poor people, but the greedy moneylenders lent money at interest when they ought not to. The greedy moneylenders are hunched over, looking at the moneybags that hang from their neck.

Finally, the sodomites took something that ought to be fertile and made it infertile. Instead of having sex of a kind that results in children, they had sex of a kind that can never result in children. For this sin, they run continuously in groups with other sodomites.

All of these groups are violent against God. God is not a physical person (except in the case of the Incarnation), so someone may ask, How can a sinner be violent against God?

Blasphemers are violent against God directly. They curse God directly. The greedy moneylenders and the sodomites are violent against God indirectly. The greedy moneylenders take advantage of the poor, although God has several commandments saying to take care of the poor, not harm them. The sodomites are against God in that they are going against the commandment to "Be fruitful and multiply."

Virgil said to Dante, "Now let us continue our journey. The wood lines the desert. Stay in the wood and do not set foot on the burning sand."

They walked on until they reached a stream of reddish water. This was a branch from the river of boiling blood. Its bed and banks were made of stone, and it crossed the burning, infertile desert.

"This stream is our way across the burning desert," Virgil said to Dante. "Above it, the falling flakes of flame are put out. This stream is the most remarkable sight you have yet seen in Hell."

Intrigued by Virgil, Dante asked him to explain more about the stream.

"In the Mediterranean is an island called Crete," Virgil said, "and on that island is the place where Rhea hid Jupiter, her son, from his father, Saturn, a monster who usually devoured his children. Whenever the young Jupiter cried, Rhea ordered her servants to shout loudly to conceal Jupiter's presence from his cannibalistic father.

"A statue of an old man is located on Crete. The Old Man of Crete is made of many kinds of materials, which grow less in quality descending from the head to the feet. The Old Man's head is made of gold, his arms and shoulders and chest are made of silver, the rest of his torso is made of brass, and his legs and one foot are made of iron. His other foot — the right one — is made of baked clay."

Virgil thought, *And so it is with the ages of man. At first there was a golden age, which was followed by a silver age, which was followed by other ages that became successively more degraded.*

Virgil continued, "The Old Man of Crete shows his back to the Egyptian seaport Damietta, symbol of the pagan world. The Old Man of Crete faces Rome, home of the Pope and symbol of the Christian world.

"Except for the golden head, the statue is flawed. The eyes of the statue drip tears. The tears flow to the ground and become the streams and rivers and pools of the Inferno. These are those streams and rivers and pools:

"The Acheron, over which Charon ferries the souls of the dead.

"The Styx, a marsh in which the angry and the sullen and the slothful are punished.

"The Phlegethon, a name that means fiery.

"The Cocytus, which you will later see for yourself."

Dante asked, "You did not mention the Lethe, and when will I see the Phlegethon?"

Virgil replied, "You have already seen the Phlegethon, which was the river of boiling blood in which the physically violent were punished.

"You will see the Lethe later, but not in Hell. It is in a place where those who have purged themselves of sin gather to wash.

"Now it is time to move on. Stay by me, and stay by the stream. Above the stream the flakes of falling flames are put out."

Chapter 15: Brunetto Latini

As Dante and Virgil continued walking, Dante observed the burning desert. He saw that the stone bank of the river was like a wall built in a country below sea level to keep sea water out of a field so that it could be used to grow crops. In that case, the walls make the field fertile rather than infertile. Here in the burning desert, of course, the wall is unable to make the burning desert fertile.

Virgil and Dante had left the wood of the suicides far behind, and now one of the groups of running sinners were coming towards them.

These are some of the sodomites, Virgil thought. *They are men who sought sex with other men. They took something that ought to be fertile and made it infertile.*

The men looked at Dante the way that some men will look at other men at night, and one of the sodomites recognized Dante and touched the hem of his clothing and shouted, "This is a marvel!"

Dante looked closely at the burned features of the sodomite, recognized him as a man he had known and still respected, and said, "Is this really you here, Sir?"

This is Brunetto Latini, Virgil thought. *This sodomite was famous for his writings, including the* Trésor, *which recounted much encyclopedic knowledge of his day. After the Battle of Montaperti in 1260, he was exiled from Florence. In addition to being a scholar, he was a Guelf.*

You have something to learn here, Dante. You do not have homosexual feelings, yet you have something to learn from Brunetto Latini. He was a scholar, but he was very concerned with becoming famous through his writing. You, Dante, need to be more concerned with telling the truth in your writing than with becoming famous through your writing.

You, Dante, are in the Inferno to learn things that will keep you out of the Inferno. What you need to learn here is to not take something that should be fertile and make it infertile. This, of course, is what the sodomites do. No amount of homosexual intercourse will result in the birth of a baby from that union.

Souls in the Inferno know the future, and so I know that you will later be engaged in what should be a fertile act: the writing of The Divine Comedy. *To make that work fertile, you must tell the truth in it. What could make the act of writing* The Divine Comedy *infertile? If you write in order to become famous instead of writing in order to say the truth,* The Divine Comedy *will not be the fertile work of art that it could and should be.*

Brunetto said to Dante, "If it is OK with you, I would like to talk to you for a while, while I let the rest of my group run on ahead."

Dante replied, "I would like that. Please stay a while and talk to me, as long as my companion here does not mind."

"I will, then," Brunetto said, "but I must keep on running beside you. Any of my group who stops for even a moment is condemned to lie on the burning sand for a hundred years, and he is unable to brush the burning flakes of fire from his body during that time."

Dante continued walking, but he kept his head low to show respect to his friend. Of course, he did not dare to step onto the burning sand.

"You are still alive, so why are you here?" Brunetto asked. "You obviously have an impressive destiny. Who is your guide?"

"In the living world, I lost my way," Dante said. "I have been trying to find my way to the right path, and yesterday this soul appeared to serve as my guide. This path through Hell is actually the right path to lead me to the path I ought to be on."

Way to go, Dante, Virgil thought. *You no longer think that your great genius is responsible for your being here, although Brunetto seems to think that. Instead, you realize that you so messed up your life that this journey is necessary to save your soul.*

"Dante, you are gifted," Brunetto said. "You are going to be famous. Your name will be in lights. I saw that clearly when I was alive, and if I had not died when I did, I would have continued to encourage you.

"But not everyone feels about you the way that I do. Some people are your enemies. You will do good deeds, but those people will not recognize them. They will make your life hard. Do not allow them to keep you from your destiny and from the fame that ought to be yours."

"I wish that you were still alive," Dante replied. "When you were alive, you taught me how people can make themselves eternal."

Be careful, Dante, Virgil thought. *You say that Brunetto taught you how people can make themselves eternal. That is a reference to becoming famous on Earth through writing.*

Yet Brunetto is in Hell for all eternity. Brunetto did not teach you about the right kind of "eternal." Brunetto was all about gaining eternal fame on Earth, not eternal life in Heaven.

If you, Dante, were to concentrate on becoming famous rather than telling the truth in The Divine Comedy, *you may end up like Brunetto, with fame that is not long lasting on Earth and with punishment that is eternal in the Inferno.*

If you, Dante, were to concentrate on becoming famous rather than telling the truth in The Divine Comedy, *you might not put Popes in Hell, but instead flatter them so that you could be their guests and drop their names to other people.*

If you, Dante, were to concentrate on becoming famous rather than telling the truth in The Divine Comedy, *you might not put any of your friends in your* Inferno, *but instead you might put only your enemies in your* Inferno.

Dante continued talking to Brunetto, "I will write down your prophecy about the enemies who will want to hurt me. A Heavenly lady will be able to make clearer to me all that you have said. I have heard other prophecies that she can also interpret."

Virgil, pleased that Dante had listened carefully to what had been said to him, repeated a proverb to Dante, "He listens well who notes well what he hears."

Dante then asked Brunetto about some of the other sinners with him.

Brunetto replied that many clerics and many men of letters were in his group. By name he mentioned Francesco d'Accorso, a lawyer from Florence who also had taught law at the University of Bologna, and Andrea de' Mozzi, who from 1287 to 1295 had been the Bishop of Florence.

Then Brunetto said, "I would like to stay and talk with you longer, but I cannot. The dust rising from the desert over there shows that a new group of sinners is arriving, and I must not mingle with them.

"I do ask of you one thing: Remember my *Trésor*. On it my fame rests."

Then Brunetto, a naked sinner, raced away the way a naked runner at Verona would compete in a race. He ran quickly, as if he would take the first prize.

I hope that you, Dante, have learned what you ought to have learned, Virgil thought. *Brunetto truly has a keen interest in fame. However, compromising your artistic vision for fame is a sin. If you don't tell the truth in your art, your art will not live on and it will not positively affect other people.*

Ironically, if you do tell the truth in your art, it can live on and positively affect other people, and your fame will be greater than if you had compromised your artistic vision. You, Dante, may be remembered as one of the greatest poets who ever lived. At best, Brunetto will be a footnote in future scholarly volumes. If you achieve your destiny, Dante, and if you resist writing simply in order to be famous, anyone who reads the Trésor *hundreds of years from now will read it only in the hope that he or she will learn more about you, Dante.*

Books should be fertile; books written only to make the writer famous are infertile.

Chapter 16: The Violent Against Nature (Continued)

Now Dante and Virgil could hear a waterfall in the distance, indicating that they were approaching the boundary of this Circle and would have to soon find a way down to the next Circle: Circle 8.

At this point three sodomites saw Dante and broke away from their group and started running toward him, shouting, "By your clothing, you seem to come from our city: polluted Florence! Stop and speak with us for a while."

Dante looked at them and saw their wounds from the falling flakes of flame. Some wounds were old, and many wounds were new. Clearly, these souls had suffered and were suffering.

Virgil heard the shout and looked at the three sinners coming toward Dante and him. He told Dante, "I recognize these sinners, and they are worthy of your respect. If not for the burning plain, *you* should be running toward *them*."

The three sodomites arrived, and they formed a circle and kept running to avoid the punishment of lying on the sand for 100 years, unable to brush away the flames from their body. In the circle they moved the way that a professional wrestler, oiled and naked, will move as he looks over his opponent to see which grip will be best before the real wrestling action begins. As they ran in the circle, each sinner kept his eyes on Dante.

"If our punishment makes you less willing to speak to us," one sinner said, "perhaps our great fame on Earth will lead you to speak with us. We would like to know who you are, and how you — a living man — are able to walk through Hell.

"The sinner is front of me is Guido Guerra, a warrior and adviser. In 1260, the Florentine Guelfs attacked Siena at Montaperti. Before the battle, Guido Guerra advised the Florentine Guelfs not to attack Siena.

"The sinner behind me is Tegghiaio Aldobrandi, who also advised the Florentine Guelfs not to attack Siena at Montaperti. He knew that many mercenaries had joined the Sienese forces and therefore were very likely to be victorious in the battle.

"As all Florentines now know, they should have accepted these men's advice. The Sienese won the Battle of Montaperti and routed the Guelfs. Farinata, who is punished among the heretics, was one of the generals of the Sienese and their allied forces.

"I am Jacopo Rusticucci, and I was wealthy. My wife was unpleasant, and I sent her home to her father. She was reluctant to do what I wanted her to do, and I blame my sodomy on her."

Dante knew the biographies of these sinners, and he respected them. Guilty they were of sodomy, but they had been good patriots who loved Florence and wanted the best for her, just like Dante. He would have joined them, but the burning sand prevented him from going to them.

Dante said to the sinners, "I feel grief for the punishment you are suffering. As you think, I am from Florence, your city, and I have heard much about you and about your love for her and about your accomplishments.

"I am on a journey to a better place, but first I must walk through Hell, going down to the very center of the Earth and thus to the bottom of the Inferno."

"Please tell us about Florence," Jacopo Rusticucci requested. "Are Florentines filled with courtesy and valor, or are these qualities no longer found in the city?

"We have heard from a newly arrived sinner, Guglielmo Borsiere, that Florence is in bad shape."

"You have heard truly," Dante said. "Newly rich people encourage pride and encourage unrestraint and make Florence weep."

All three sinners said, "Thank you for so clearly answering the question. You are fortunate in being able to speak so clearly and so well. If you are equally fortunate in being able to return to the Land of the Living, keep our memory alive among living men."

The three sinners then raced to rejoin their group.

Virgil and Dante continued walking, and the sound of the waterfall grew much louder, making it difficult for them to hear what the other spoke. They had reached the pit again and needed to go down to the next Circle.

Dante wore a cord around his waist to serve as a belt, much as the Franciscans did. He had thought earlier to use it to catch the leopard that was keeping him in the dark wood of error and keeping him from ascending to the light — his self-confidence was too abundant and too foolish then.

Virgil requested that cord, and Dante untied it and handed it to him. Virgil then threw it into the abyss.

Dante thought, *We will see something strange soon. The cord is a signal.*

Virgil has many powers. One power is to always know what time it is by the location of the heavenly bodies such as the Sun and the Moon and the planets even though the Inferno is always dark. Another is great strength. And yet another is to know what Dante is thinking.

Virgil said to Dante, "As you think, soon you will see something strange — something that will respond to my signal." Almost immediately, Dante saw a figure rising from below through the air. The figure appeared to be swimming in the air.

Chapter 17: Geryon

"Behold the monster that makes the world stink!" Virgil said to Dante as he motioned for the monster to land.

And the monster — the embodiment of fraud — did land.

Dante and Virgil saw the guard of the Circles dedicated to punishing fraud: Geryon, a creature with a face like that of an honest man, a body made of a combination of parts of beasts, and a stinging tail like that of a scorpion.

Geryon has three parts, Virgil noted. *Like other triune guards, Geryon is a perversion of the Holy Trinity.*

Geryon is an appropriate guard of Circle 8 because he embodies fraud. His honest-looking face encourages people to trust him, while he hides his tail that will sting his victim. Geryon usually stings the sinners who ride on his back, but he won't do that to Dante and me. When Geryon first gets sinners to trust him and then he stings them with his scorpion's tail, he commits fraud.

Look at Geryon. He is displaying his honest-looking face, but he is trying to keep his stinging tail out of sight; it is hanging down the cliff leading to the next Circle. He is trying to commit fraud even as I look at him.

Geryon provides transportation to the next Circle. Minos flings sinners down into Hell, but at least some sinners must travel further down to the Circle where they will be punished. Just as Phlegyas the ferryman takes sinners across the Styx, so Geryon flies sinners from Circle 7 to Circle 8.

Dante was surprised by the way the monster looked. His face made you want to trust him, but the rest of him was animalistic. He had clawed paws, not hands. He had hairy legs instead of arms. His back, his belly, and his flanks seemed to be painted with exotic designs like those of some snakes. And he had a stinging tail like that of a scorpion, although he was attempting to keep it out of sight.

"Now we need to go to the evil beast," Virgil said to Dante. They did, being careful to stay off the burning sand. Dante looked around and saw some sinners close to the edge of the burning sand.

Virgil noticed Dante looking at the sinners and told him, "Go and see them. That will complete your knowledge of the torments in this Circle. But don't stay long. I will be here convincing the evil beast — whose name is Geryon — to take us down to Circle 8."

Dante walked toward the sinners, who were in pain because of the flakes of flame falling from the sky onto them and because of the burning sand on which they crouched. Their hands moved constantly, brushing off flames and trying to provide some protection from the burning sand. They resembled dogs trying unsuccessfully to get relief from fleas as they constantly scratched here and scratched there.

Because when they were alive, the greedy moneylenders took something that ought to be infertile and made it fertile, now that they are dead, they are in this burning plain with fire raining down on them. Here they are bent over, just like living greedy moneylenders who bend over their tables and count their money. Hanging from the necks of these sinners in Hell are moneybags, which they gaze at greedily just as they did while they were living.

Dante looked carefully at the faces of several sinners, but he recognized no one, although he knew that the sinners were greedy moneylenders because of the moneybags that were hanging from their necks. These sinners' love of money had kept them from accomplishing something great in the Land of the Living. Because they were undistinguished in the Land of the Living, they cannot be distinguished in the Land of the Dead.

However, although Dante could not recognize any individual greedy moneylenders, he did recognize the families that the greedy moneylenders came from by looking the designs — the coats of arms — on their moneybags. He identified a member of the Gianfigliazzi family of Florence because the sinner had a yellow purse that was decorated with a blue lion. He identified a member of the Ubriachi family of Florence because the sinner had a red purse that was decorated with a goose. And he identified a member of the Scrovegni family of Padua because the sinner had a purse that was decorated with a blue sow.

The sinner who was a member of the Scrovegni family told Dante, "What are you looking at! Get away from me! What are you doing here!

"But since you are alive, I will tell you that soon my neighbor Vitaliano will arrive here in this Circle of Hell and sit on my left. We will then have one more Paduan among all these Florentines."

The Paduan then stuck his tongue out at Dante, who returned to Virgil lest he anger his guide by staying too long.

Virgil, who was already sitting on the back of Geryon, told Dante, "Now is the time for courage and strength. This is our transportation to the next Circle. Sit in front of me so that I will be between you and this monster's stinging scorpion's tail."

Dante was afraid, but he obeyed Virgil and mounted Geryon's back. He thought about asking Virgil to hold on to him, and Virgil, reading Dante's mind, did just that.

Virgil then ordered the monster, "Geryon, take flight, and fly gently. Remember, on your back is a living person."

Geryon launched himself in flight and descended.

Dante was afraid. He thought, *I am more afraid than Phaëthon was when he took flight. Phaëthon was Apollo's son, but he was born to a mortal woman, and so he was a mortal. One day, he journeyed to see his father, who wanted to give him a gift — a gift consisting of anything he wanted. Phaëthon decided that he wanted to drive his father's chariot. Apollo was the Sun-god, and he drove the chariot that warmed and lit the Earth. However, Apollo knew that only a god could handle the horses that drove the chariot, and he begged his son to choose another gift. However, Phaëthon was determined to drive the chariot. Since Apollo had sworn an inviolable oath by the River Styx, he had to let Phaëthon drive the chariot.*

As Apollo had foreknown, Phaëthon could not control the horses, and the chariot drove wildly over the sky, coming too close to the Earth sometimes and going too far away from the Earth sometimes. Eventually, the chariot came so close to the Earth that the Earth was about to catch fire. Fortunately for the people living on the Earth, Jupiter killed Phaëthon with a thunderbolt and Apollo was able to drive the chariot again, and so everything went back to normal.

I am even more afraid than Icarus, Daedalus' son, was when he fell out of the sky. Icarus was the son of Daedalus. Daedalus built the wooden cow that Pasiphaë crept into when she fell in love with a bull and wanted the bull to make love to her. After Pasiphaë gave birth to the Minotaur, Daedalus built the labyrinth that housed the Minotaur.

To make sure that no one could ever learn the secret of how to get out of the labyrinth, the King of Crete imprisoned Daedalus and Icarus, his son. Daedalus fashioned wings made out of wax and feathers so that he and his son could fly away from the island where they were imprisoned. Daedalus warned his son not to fly too high, for if he did the Sun would melt the wax, the feathers would fall out of the wings, and he would fall into the sea and drown.

That is exactly what happened. Icarus became excited because he was flying, he flew too high, the wax of his wings melted, and he fell into the sea and drowned.

Dante and Virgil could hear the roaring of the waterfall as they descended. Dante looked out at the terrain of Circle 8 as they descended, but leaning outward frightened him so much that he quickly stopped doing it.

Geryon was angry at Dante and Virgil because he had expected to be able to torment some newly arrived sinners when he answered the signal of the cord that had been used by Dante as a belt.

When Geryon descended in spirals from Circle 7 to Circle 8, he was like a falcon that was angry at its master. When Geryon landed, he made sure to land in such a way that Virgil and Dante were almost up against the jagged cliff.

And as soon as Virgil and Dante got off his back, Geryon took off like an arrow shot from a bowstring, getting away from Dante and Virgil as quickly as possible.

Chapter 18: Panders and Seducers; Flatterers

At this point, Dante had seen seven of the nine Circles of the Inferno, as well as the Vestibule of Hell, where the uncommitted were punished. He had seen the first Circle of Hell: Limbo, the residence of the virtuous pagans and the unbaptized. He had seen the four Circles (2-5) devoted to punishing the sinners who were guilty of incontinence in lust, gluttony, hoarding money and wasting money, and anger. He had seen Circle 6, which is devoted to punishing the sinners who are guilty of heresy. And he had seen Circle 7, which punishes the violent in three different areas: 1) The river of boiling blood punishes the physically violent, 2) The grubby wood punishes the suicides, and it punishes those who had violently wasted their wealth and then courted death, and 3) The burning desert punishes those who were directly violent against God through blasphemy, those who were indirectly violent against God by doing violence to Nature, which had been created by God, through sodomy, and those who were indirectly violent against God by doing violence through rejecting God's laws regarding lending money at interest.

Now only two Circles remained. Circle 8 punishes those sinners who are guilty of simple fraud. Fraud involves the willful use of misrepresentation to deprive another person of his or her rights. For example, someone can claim to be able to foretell the future and charge people money to be told the future. Simple fraud is fraud, but it is not committed against those to whom one has a special obligation of trust.

Circle 9 punishes the worst sinners of all: those who are guilty of complex fraud. Complex fraud is fraud committed against those to whom one has a special obligation of trust. Sinners who commit complex fraud are traitors of various kinds: e.g., traitors to kin/family, traitors to government, traitors to guests, or traitors to God.

As Dante and Virgil descended from Circle 7 to Circle 8 on the back of Geryon, Dante had an aerial view of Circle 8. He saw that it was divided into 10 ditches or valleys or pockets that are known as the Malebolge, a plural word that means "evil pockets" or "evil pouches." They may be called that because the sinners here regard everything as being for sale. They wish to pocket money.

Each Malebolgia punishes a different kind of sinner who committed simple fraud, and some Malebolge punish two kinds of sinners whose sins are related.

Dante remembered what Virgil had told him earlier about Circle 8:

"Ten kinds of sinners engage in simple fraud:

"One, Seducers and Panders,

"Two, Flatterers,

"Three, Simonists,

"Four, Fortune-Tellers and Sorcerers,

"Five, Grafters — those who give or accept bribes,

"Six, Hypocrites,

"Seven, Thieves,

"Eight, Evil Deceivers/Those Who Misuse Great Gifts,

"Nine, Schismatics — those who cause divisions (in families, in politics, in religion, etc.), and

"Ten, Falsifiers, including Counterfeiters."

As Dante looked around as Geryon descended in circles, he noticed that bridges crossed over the Malebolge like the spokes of a wheel; however, he could see that at least one bridge over the sixth evil pocket was broken — he did not have time to look at all of the bridges.

After Dante and Virgil had gotten off Geryon's back and Geryon had sped away, they walked to see the sinners in the first evil pocket. Here Dante saw his first horned devils of the Inferno. They were cruelly whipping the naked sinners as they walked, and they rejoiced in their work.

Dante saw a face that seemed familiar, so he looked closely at him. The sinner saw him and lowered his face in an attempt to keep from being recognized, but Dante recognized him anyway.

Virgil thought, *The sinners deep in the Inferno have committed worse sins than those who are high in the Inferno. For this reason, many of them don't want to be remembered on Earth. And, of course, misrepresentation is a part of fraud. These sinners may be trying to keep whatever good reputation they have on Earth.*

Dante said to the sinner, "I know you. You are Venedico Caccianemico. Why are you being punished in this evil pocket?"

Venedico Caccianemico knew that he had been recognized and that Dante would soon know his story even if he said nothing, so he answered Dante's question: "I used my own sister to advance myself. I let the Marquis of Este sleep with my sister, who was named Ghisolabella. As you can now tell, I am a pander.

"I am from the city of Bologna, and many more people from my city are here."

A devil whipped Venedico Caccianemico's back and told him, "Keep walking! No women are here for pimps like you to sell."

Dante and Virgil moved on and saw a second group of sinners walking in the opposite direction that the first group was walking. The first group of sinners consisted of panders or pimps; the second group of sinners consisted of seducers. The two sins are related in that both involve unethical sex, and so both kinds of sinners are punished in the first Malebolge.

Virgil told Dante, "Look at the imposing sinner coming toward us. He suffers pain, but he does not cry. He is Jason, of Jason and the Argonauts fame. He set out in the *Argo*, the first ship, to find the Golden Fleece, and he achieved his objective. He is a seducer. As a seducer he would sleep with women and then abandon them when he found it convenient to do so. He slept with Hypsipyle, and then he abandoned her when she was pregnant. She had twins. He married and had children with Medea, but then he abandoned her when someone he thought was better came along: Creusa, the daughter of Creon, the King of Corinth. Medea killed the children she had had with Jason in response.

"We have seen enough here. These sinners caused pain to others, and now they feel pain. Let us move on."

On the bridge crossing the second evil pocket, Dante and Virgil looked down at the sinners in the pocket, from which was arising a nauseating stench, and there they saw the flatterers. While they were alive, out of their mouths had come metaphorical crap: flattery. Now that they were dead in Hell, they were covered with literal crap: human excrement.

Dante saw a sinner's head that was so covered with crap that he was unable to tell if the sinner were a priest or a layman.

The sinner shouted at Dante, "Why do you stare at me more than at these other sinners?"

Dante knew the man then, and he replied, "I know you. You are Alessio Interminei from Lucca, and while you were alive you were known for your flattery."

Alessio Interminei replied, "Because of my continual flatteries while I was alive, I am stuck in this evil pocket."

Virgil then said to Dante, "Look at this woman here. She is scratching herself with her shitty fingernails — please forgive my use of this kind of language, for it is quite appropriate in Hell. This woman is Thaïs the whore, who flattered her lover when he asked whether he deserved her thanks after he gave her a gift. She told him, 'You incredibly deserve my thanks.'

"We have seen enough here. Let us move on."

Chapter 19: The Simonists

Simon Magus, you are among the worst sinners who have ever existed, as are your followers, Dante the Poet thought. *You were the first to try to engage in the sin of simony, the buying and selling of church offices and spiritual benefits for money. I have read about you in* Acts 8. *Peter and John were using one of the gifts of God: the laying on of hands to convey the Holy Spirit. You, Simon Magus, were impressed by this and wanted to pay Peter and John money to teach you how to do that. Of course, Peter and John were insulted because the laying on of hands to convey the Holy Spirit is a free gift of God and is not for sale. They asked you to repent your sin.*

Your followers also try to buy things that are not for sale. Someone who wants to become a bishop can do so by paying money to dishonest and corrupt people with power. Such people ought not to become bishops.

Why would someone want to buy a church office? They would look at it as an investment. They would be paying money to gain power and perhaps to gain more money. However, are these the people who should be in church offices? Do we want a Pope who has bought his way into that position? The answer is no. We prefer someone who deserves the position through his own merit. We prefer a meritocracy to a plutocracy.

The trouble with simony is that the people who deserve church offices because of their merit don't get them. Either they don't have the money to buy the church office, or they do have the money but won't buy the church office because they know that simony is wrong.

Dante the Pilgrim and Virgil had reached the third pocket, where the simonists are punished. Dante would rejoice when he found out how the simonists are punished in the third pocket of Circle 8.

Standing on the bridge above the third pocket, Dante looked down and saw a number of holes in the rock. The holes resembled the holes where priests would stand in a baptistery as they baptized people.

Dante remembered, *I once smashed a baptistery, not as an action against the Church, but because a child was drowning in it. Rumors arose, however, that I was being sacrilegious.*

Of course, Virgil knew what Dante was thinking — he had that power. Virgil thought, *Anyone seeing Dante smash the baptistery would of course think that he was being sacrilegious, but of course he was saving a life, an action that his religion definitely approves of. Similarly, when a prophet criticizes some immoral practices of his religion, he may be seen as being sacrilegious, but of course he is not. The prophet is trying to make the practices of his religion better by criticizing immoral practices such as simony. If Dante tells the truth when he writes* The Divine Comedy, *he will criticize the bad practices of the Church as a way to make the Church reform itself and become better.*

Dante saw legs sticking out of the holes in the rock. Flames were dancing on the sinners' feet; some of the flames were redder and hotter than other flames. The sinners in those holes were worse than the other sinners.

Dante asked Virgil, "Which sinner is that whose feet are burned by a hotter flame than the feet of the other sinners?"

Virgil replied, "The way down is steep, but I am strong and surefooted, so if you wish, I will carry you down there so that you may ask the sinner who he is and why he is here."

Dante was agreeable, and when they had reached the sinner, Dante asked, "Wretched soul, what are you? If you can speak, speak, if you are able."

The soul mistook Dante for the soul of a sinner who would die three years later and be punished here: "Are you here already, Pope Boniface VIII? According to the Book of Fate, you are not supposed to die until 1303. Have you grown tired of engaging in simony and of tearing apart the Church?"

Dante was surprised by what the sinner had said, so he remained quiet, but Virgil advised him, "Tell the sinner that he is mistaken, that you are not who he thinks you are."

Dante did as Virgil advised, and the sinner said, "What do you want? If you want to know my name, I am the son of the she-bear; that is, I am a member of the Orsini family. When I became Pope, I did not truly take a new name and leave my family behind to serve a new, greater family, even though people called me Pope Nicholas III. Instead, I kept the name of Orsini, and I used my position to advance the interests of my Orsini relatives. When I was alive, I was greedy to pocket wealth, and now that I am dead, I myself am pocketed.

"Under me are many other simonists. Soon, Pope Boniface VIII will arrive here and he will push me deeper in this hole just as my arrival here pushed other simonists deeper in this hole. Later, another simonist, Pope Clement V, will arrive and push Pope Boniface VIII and me and the other simonists here in this hole deeper."

Dante was angry. He knew how bad is the sin of simony. He said sarcastically to Pope Nicholas III, "Exactly how much money did Peter have to pay to Jesus to get the keys to the gates of Heaven? I believe that he had to pay no money, but simply follow Jesus. How much money did Matthias have to pay to Peter and the other apostles to take Judas' place? I believe that he had to pay no money, but simply to do God's will.

"You deserve your punishment, for your sin is so great. You supported the side that paid the most money, so enjoy the reward you gained.

"Your sin of simony brings grief to the Church and to the world. It hurts the good, and it makes the bad happy.

"Your god is made of gold and silver coins. You are like an idolater, except that an idolater worships one idol, while you worship hundreds of idols."

Then to himself, but loud enough for others to hear, Dante said, "Constantine, you meant well, but your gift of money and wealth to the Church helped make it corrupt!"

Constantine was the first Christian Roman emperor, Virgil thought. *When he moved from Rome to the city of Constantinople, he supposedly gave much power and material possessions to the Pope. The medieval belief was that Constantine deliberately moved East in order to reward Pope Sylvester with power and possessions because Pope Sylvester had cured him of leprosy. Dante believes that this Donation of Constantinople corrupted many Popes and the Church.*

As a soul in the Inferno, I know the future. Actually, the so-called Donation of Constantine is a forgery, but this will be proved long after Dante's day; not until the 15th century will the so-called Donation of Constantine be proved to be a forgery.

Pope Nicholas III's feet kicked harder than ever, perhaps out of anger or perhaps because he knew that Dante's criticism was justified.

Assassins are punished by being buried alive, Dante thought. *I have seen assassins try to put off dying a few more moments by calling to a priest to come back so that they can confess one more sin. Anyone seeing us here could think that I am a priest and this sinner is an assassin. And this sinner really is an assassin. By engaging in simony, this sinner is an assassin of the Church.*

This punishment is a parody of a number of things. It is a parody of baptism. Baptism is done with water, not with fire. And it is a parody of the Pentecost, in which fire came down from above and sat on the heads of the followers of Jesus and they were able to speak in tongues.

In addition, the way the sinners are stuck headfirst in the hole is a reminder of how Simon Magus died. In the Acts of Peter, I have read about Simon Magus' death. Simon became a magician, and he learned to fly. Magus, of course, means magician. Simon was flying and criticizing the one true God, so Saint Peter prayed for Simon to fall, and he fell. The way these sinners are stuck headfirst in the hole resembles an image of Simon Magus falling and hitting the ground headfirst.

I can certainly understand why you sinners are upside down here. You sinners are upside down because you placed things upside down in the living world — you placed material things before spiritual things, thus upsetting their proper order.

Dante noticed that Virgil was smiling.

Dante, this is a job well done, Virgil thought. *Your opinion of the sin of simony is exactly right. You started this journey naïve, but you are wising up.*

Virgil picked Dante up and carried him up out of the pocket. When he had carried Dante down into the ditch, he had carried Dante at his side. Now, because he was pleased with Dante, he hugged him to his chest.

Dante and Virgil walked to the next pocket.

Chapter 20: The Soothsayers and Fortune Tellers

Dante and Virgil now were on the bridge above the fourth bolgia. Looking down, Dante saw that the sinners were crying as they walked around the Circle; the floor of the Circle was wet with tears. Dante also saw that the sinners were twisted in a grotesque way; their heads were twisted so that the face was above the back, not above the chest. As the sinners cried, their tears ran down their backs and into the cleft of their buttocks.

Dante cried, too — something that Virgil did not like.

Dante is a backslider, Virgil thought. *He realized that simony is a great sin indeed, but now he pities how the sinners are being punished in the fourth bolgia.*

"Dante, you are a fool," Virgil said. "The Inferno is not a place for pity. Every soul here deserves to be here, and every soul here is punished in a very appropriate way.

"The sinners in this fourth bolgia are the soothsayers and the fortune tellers. They tried to look too far ahead in the future, and now they are punished by not being able to look ahead at all. Now they travel by walking backward because they can see only backward, not forward.

"Look around you. Here is a sinner who was one of the Seven Against Thebes. The two sons of Oedipus, Eteocles and Polynices, decided to share the rule of Thebes after their father abdicated the throne. Each brother was supposed to rule for a year and then allow the other brother to take the throne for a year; however, after ruling for a year, Eteocles refused to step down from the throne and allow Polynices to rule for a year. Therefore, Polynices raised an army and marched against Thebes and his brother.

"Amphiaraus was one of the seven generals of the army marching against Thebes and Eteocles. He foresaw that he would die if he fought against Thebes, so he attempted to hide himself so that he would not have to fight. However, his wife revealed his hiding place, so he had to go on the military expedition. During the attack on Thebes, the Earth opened up and he fell into the chasm, dying as he had foreseen. He appeared before Minos, who never errs. Minos judged him and sent him here.

"Now look at Tiresias, the most famous prophet of Thebes. You have read about him in Book Three of Ovid's *Metamorphoses*. Tiresias was famous enough to be consulted by Odysseus in the Underworld in Homer's *Odyssey*.

"Tiresias lived life as both a man and a woman. He once saw two snakes having sex, and he hit them with his staff. As his punishment, Juno turned him into a woman. Tiresias married and gave birth to Manto, his daughter, who was also a prophet. After seven years as a woman, he again saw two snakes having sex, and he again hit them with his staff and changed sexes, this time turning back into a man. Because Tiresias had lived life as both a man and a woman, when Jupiter and Juno quarreled over who enjoyed sex more — the man or the woman — they turned to Tiresias to settle the argument. Tiresias said that women enjoyed sex more, and Juno struck him blind.

"Because Tiresias tried to see too far into the future, he is punished here.

"Now look at Tiresias' daughter, Manto, whose long hair now covers her breasts instead of her back, while her hairy parts are now in back and not in front. Manto was a soothsayer at Thebes. After Tiresias died, she went to Italy and founded Mantua, the city where I, Virgil, was born.

"Listen carefully, and I will tell you the true story of how my city, Mantua, was founded. Truth is important, and I don't want you to believe any inaccurate stories of how Mantua was founded.

"Manto saw land lying surrounded mostly by a marsh. She moved there and died there. After she died, men arrived and built a town there because it was well protected by the marsh. They named their town after Manto."

Learn from this story, Virgil thought. *The theme of my story is truth. The story of the founding of Mantua is controversial, with more than one version. I am here telling the true story. Truth, of course, is something that people engaging in fraud wish to hide.*

You, Dante, must say the truth in your writing. If you tell the true story of the founding of Mantua in your Divine Comedy, *you will be letting your readers know that you care about truth. You will be establishing your credibility. Because your readers will know that you care about the truth of the founding of Mantua, they will know that you are careful to report the truth about the afterlife.*

"Virgil," Dante said, "you always tell me the truth. Now can you tell me about some other sinners here?"

Virgil replied, "Eurypylus is punished here in this part of the Inferno. You know about him from reading my *Aeneid* — my epic poem that you know almost by heart. Eurypylus was a Greek warrior who was sent to the Oracle of Delphi in order to inquire why the gods were angry at the Greeks.

"Also punished here is Michael Scot, a mathematician and scholar who was born in Scotland. He was a magician who was able to serve his guests food magically brought from France and Spain and other countries.

"But we have seen enough. Let us continue our journey."

Chapter 21: The Grafters

Arriving at the fifth pocket, Dante noticed a strange darkness. A dark pitch or tar was boiling in the pocket the way that dark pitch boiled when the Venetians repaired their ships during the winter when they could not sail. Here boiling bubbles popped in the pitch.

Always on the lookout, Virgil said to Dante, "Watch out!" He stood by Dante, who looked up and saw a frightening black devil coming along the ridge. The devil had wings and moved quickly, and he was carrying the soul of a sinner.

The devil shouted, "Hey, Malebranche, here's another sinner, one of the elders of Santa Zita. Plenty more grafters are coming to be punished here. Stick him under the boiling pitch. These are the people who accept bribes to change decisions."

Graft is a bribe, Dante thought. *When I was exiled from Florence, I was unjustly accused of being a grafter. A politician who takes money to pass legislation favorable to a certain corporation is guilty of graft. A judge who takes money to rule a person innocent instead of guilty is guilty of graft. What simony is to the religious world, graft is to the secular world.*

And Virgil thought, Malebranche *is a good name for these black devils.* Malebranche *means* Evil Claws.

The black devil flung the sinner into the boiling pitch, and the sinner rose to the surface and floated on his back, with his hands outstretched as if he were being crucified. The black devil took off quickly to bring another sinner to be punished here.

The other devils saw the floating sinner and instantly jabbed him with a hundred pitchfork prongs, saying, "No floating here. Don't imitate a person on a cross. All you sinners stay below the surface of the sticky pitch so you can bake. We have grappling hooks, and if we catch you raising yourself out of the hot pitch, we will torment you."

This is another contrapasso, Virgil thought. *The grafters were sticky fingered, and so now they are sticky from the pitch in this part of the Inferno. The grafters used their political and judicial offices to take bribes and make money. As these people manipulated and tormented other people during their lives, so the demons manipulate and torment the grafters.*

Virgil also thought, *These black devils can be dangerous. I have been here before, so I know that I must be careful to protect Dante.*

As the black devils used their pitchforks to push the sinner down into the boiling tar like a cook's assistant uses a fork to push the meat down into the boiling broth so it will cook better, Virgil said to Dante, "It's best if the black devils don't yet see you. Hide yourself behind a rock. The black devils will see me, but whatever they say to me, don't worry. I have been here before, and I know how to act and what to say."

Virgil crossed the bridge, and he looked as bold and as brave as he could. The black devils saw him, and they came out from under the bridge to accost him.

Virgil shouted at them, "Behave yourselves! Let me talk to your leader before you start jabbing me with your pitchforks. After I talk to your leader, you can decide whether you still want to jab me."

The black devils all cried out, "Let Malacoda talk to him."

The black devil known as Malacoda stepped forward and said, "What good will talking to me do you?"

Virgil replied, "Do you think that I would have come so far in my journey through the Inferno if it were not the will of God? I am on a mission from God, and I have God's protection. Now that you know that, you must let me and a companion pass."

Malacoda's face fell, and he allowed his pitchfork to fall, too. He told the other black devils, "Don't harm this man."

Virgil then said to Dante, "You can come out of hiding now. We will be OK."

Dante came forward, making sure to stay close to Virgil, but to him the black devils looked threatening. He could hear them muttering to each other, saying things like, "Should I stick this pitchfork in the living person's rump?" Most of the other black devils answered, "Go ahead!"

But Malacoda, the black devil in charge of the fifth pocket, said, "Keep your hands and pitchforks off these people!"

Then he said to Virgil, "The bridge across the sixth pocket is broken here, but just ahead you will find a bridge that is still sound and that you can use to cross the pocket. The bridge was destroyed 1,066 years and one day and five hours ago."

Virgil thought, *The bridge was destroyed by the earthquake that occurred during the Harrowing of Hell. I remember when the Mighty Warrior rescued the deserving souls and took them out of Limbo.*

Malacoda continued, "I am sending some devils that way to make sure that the sinners stay deep in the boiling pitch and do not raise their backs out of the boiling bubbles to find relief from pain. You may travel with them."

Then Malacoda said to the devils, "Step forward, Alichino, Calcabrina, Cagnazzo, Libicocco, Draghignazzo, Farfarello, and Rubicante. Barbariccia will be the leader of all of you. Walk along the pocket and make sure that the sinners stay deep in the boiling pitch. Take these two to the unbroken bridge that crosses the sixth bolgia."

Dante was worried about having a pack of devils as an escort. He said to Virgil, "I don't like this. Let's travel by ourselves with no escort. Look at the devils. They mean us harm! They grind their teeth and wink at each other. We are in danger here!"

But Virgil replied, "We are safe. It is the sinners who are in danger of being tormented by the devils."

Like a military troop, the black devils saluted their leader, Malacoda, but they saluted by putting their tongue between their lips and making a farting sound.

Malacoda returned the salute by using the hole in his butt as a bugle and farting.

Malacoda *is indeed a suitable name for this black devil,* Virgil thought. Malacoda *means* Evil Tail.

Chapter 22: Ciampolo of Navarre and Deceived Demons

Dante thought, *I have seen military officers and battles and retreats. I have seen military scouts and raiding parties and tournaments. But I have never seen cavalry or infantry or ships being sent on a mission with such bugling as that of Malacoda!*

Dante and Virgil, accompanied by the black devils, continued walking on the bank along the boiling pitch. In Hell, you have to expect to see devils.

As Dante walked, he kept an eye on the sinners in the boiling pitch to see what they did. Dolphins often swim in the sea, occasionally rising to the surface and exposing their backs. Likewise, the sinners often raised their backs out of the boiling pitch momentarily to ease their pain. But quickly, like the back of a dolphin, their backs disappeared into the boiling pitch again. The sinners did not want to be captured and tormented by the Malebranche.

The sinners often, like frogs, had part of their bodies out of the boiling pitch, but when Barbariccia appeared, quickly the sinners put their entire bodies into the boiling pitch.

But one sinner was slower than the others, and Graffiacane speared him and raised him out of the boiling pitch. Dripping, the sinner looked like an otter.

The black devils were happy to have a sinner to torment. They said, "Rubicante, slice the sinner's skin off with your claws."

Dante asked Virgil, "Can you find out the name of this poor sinner who is being tormented by the black devils?"

Virgil spoke to the sinner, who replied, "I come from Navarre. My father was a spendthrift who killed himself when he ran out of money to spend. I worked for King Thibault, but I became a grafter, and now you see that I am punished here."

The punishment continued out of the boiling pitch. The two-tusked Ciriatto used one tusk to rip open the sinner's skin. The sinner was like a mouse that is being tormented by cats.

But Barbariccia, whom Malacoda had put in charge of the other devils, said, "Don't touch him — he's mine!"

Then he told Virgil, "Soon this sinner will be torn to pieces, so if you have any questions for him, ask them now."

Virgil asked the sinner, "Are any Italians in the boiling pitch with you?"

The sinner replied, "Yes, there are. Just before I was captured by these devils, I was beside an Italian — I wish that I were with him now! I would not be tormented with the hooks and claws of these devils!"

Another of the black devils, Libicocco, said, "Let's start the torment!" He then used his pitchfork to tear off a piece of the sinner's arm. Another black devil, Draghignazzo, tore off a piece of the sinner's leg, but Barbariccia glared at the black devils, and they ceased their torture.

As the sinner looked over his new wounds, Virgil asked him, "Who was the Italian you were with before you were captured?"

The sinner replied, "Gomita, the friar from Gallura, who accepted bribes to let the enemies of his lord go free. He was no petty grafter, for his grafts were huge. He spends his time talking with Michele Zanche of Logodora — but look at how the black devils grind their teeth. I would tell you more, but I am afraid of the black devils and what they are going to do to me."

Barbariccia glared at Farfarello, who was grinding his teeth, and shouted, "Stay away from the sinner!"

The sinner continued, "I can help you to talk to Tuscans and Lombards if you wish; however, for me to do that, the Malebranche must back away a little. Unless they do, the sinners in the boiling pitch won't raise their backs out of the boiling pitch, and unless the sinners do that, they can't be caught. I will help the Malebranche to capture seven Italian sinners so you can talk to them. All I have to do is whistle — that is how we signal each other that no Malebranche are around and so it is safe to raise our backs out of the boiling pitch."

Cagnazzo disbelieved the sinner: "This is a trick. Once we back away from him, he will escape us by jumping back into the boiling pitch!"

The sinner, who had not forgotten the tricks he had used to commit fraud while he was alive, said, "I certainly know tricks — especially tricks that will get my friends in trouble!"

Alichin said, "I am willing to capture seven Italian sinners. And if you try to jump, my wings will enable me to get to you quickly. We Malebranche will back away and hide."

The Malebranche did back away and hide, and the first black devil to do so was Cagnazzo, who had not believed and did not believe the sinner. Cagnazzo thought, *This sinner is playing a trick on us. He is going to jump. If he succeeds in* jumping, then the other devils and I will have an opportunity to pick a fight with Alichin, who will be responsible if this sinner gets away.

The sinner had a good sense of timing, and he jumped at exactly the best time. Alichin swooped at the sinner, trying to grab him before he hit the boiling pitch, but he failed, just as an eagle fails when he swoops at a duck, but the duck dives beneath the surface of the water.

Calcabrina took off after Alichin, hoping that the sinner would escape so that he would have an excuse to fight Alichin. As soon as the sinner dived beneath the boiling pitch, Calcabrina began to fight Alichin, who fought back, with the result that the two devils fell into the boiling pitch, befouling their wings with tar and rendering them useless for flying until they could be cleaned.

Barbariccia and four other devils set off to rescue Calcabrina and Alichin, who were being cooked in the boiling pitch. Barbariccia and the four other devils reached out with pitchforks to lift the two fallen devils from the pitch.

No fools, Dante and Virgil took the opportunity to sneak away from the black devils.

Chapter 23: The Hypocrites

As they continued their journey, Dante thought, *I remember one of the fables of Aesop: A mouse wishes to cross a pool of water, and he asks a frog to help him across the pool of water. The frog agrees to help the mouse, but halfway across the pool of water the frog attempts to drown the mouse. A hawk sees the frog and mouse, captures both of them, eats the frog, and allows the mouse to go free. Moral: The guilty are punished, and the innocent go free.*

The beginning and the moral of this fable apply to what has happened here. The black devils tried to trick us, but we are now free and two of the devils are in the boiling pitch.

But we are not out of danger yet.

Dante said to Virgil, "I fear danger. We need to hide right away. As soon as the devils fish their brothers out of the boiling pitch, they will come after us for revenge. I think I can hear them now."

Virgil replied, "I can read your thoughts. As fast as a mirror reflects your image, your thoughts are mirrored in my mind. My thoughts are the same as yours. I am looking for a place where we can slide into the next pocket."

Dante then saw the devils coming after them with their wings spread wide and flapping for more speed. Virgil also knew that the devils were coming toward them fast. He grabbed Dante the way that a mother will grab her son and rescue him from a fire — not even waiting to put something on over her underclothing. The flames are too close, and her son needs to be rescued.

Still holding Dante, Virgil slid down the bank into the next bolgia. They slid down quickly — quicker than water flows down a conduit. All the time Virgil held Dante against his chest, making sure that Dante was not hurt during the slide.

They reached the bottom of the bolgia and then looked up and saw ten black devils, but they had no need to fear the black devils: When God made the black devils the guards of the fifth pocket, He made it impossible for them to leave that pocket.

Now, in the sixth pocket, Dante and Virgil saw, slowly moving, step by step, sinners wearing gaudy clothing — clothing that weighed them down. The sinners were wearing cloaks with the hoods pulled down over their faces. These cloaks resembled the fancy cloaks that the Benedictine monks wear at Cluny. But these cloaks were gold on the outside and iron on the inside — both are heavy metals, although gold is much more valuable than iron. Weighed down by their heavy cloaks, the sinners walk slowly but everlastingly in the sixth pocket.

This is another contrapasso, Virgil thought. *These are the hypocrites, who made a show of holding beliefs that they did not actually hold. The hypocrites appeared golden on the outside although on the inside they were made of base metal, so for eternity they appropriately wear heavy cloaks that are gold on the outside but lead on the inside.*

Dante asked Virgil, "Look around, please, and see if anyone is here whom I have heard of."

Overhearing him, a sinner with a Tuscan accent called, "Don't move so quickly, and perhaps I can fulfill your request."

Virgil told Dante, "Stop and wait for the sinner, and then walk with him at his pace."

Two sinners came slowly toward Dante, and then one sinner said to the other, "Look at this man and the way his throat moves — he seems to be alive. But if both of these men here are dead, why aren't they wearing the cloak of the hypocrites?"

Then the two sinners asked Dante, "Who are you?" Dante answered, "I was born and raised in Florence, but who are you, who cry with grief?"

"We are hypocrites," said one of the sinners, "and these cloaks that are gold on the outside and iron on the inside — as we were in life — weigh us down and make our joints creak.

"I am the Guelf Catalano and my companion is the Ghibelline Loderingo. We are the Jovial Friars who were brought into Florence to help keep the peace, but instead we took sides and increased the violence of Florence. You can see that we were hypocrites: We pretended to be peacekeepers but actually we fomented violence."

Dante was going to say more, but suddenly he stopped because he saw something surprising on the ground: a figure who was crucified with three stakes.

Friar Catalano saw what Dante was looking at, and he explained, "The figure crucified on the ground is Caiaphas, who allowed Jesus to be killed even though he believed Him to be innocent. Now all the hypocrites must step on him as they make the round of this Circle. Also crucified in this way are his father-in-law, Annas, who delivered Jesus to him, and all the other Jews who advised that Jesus die."

Dante noticed that Virgil was staring, amazed, at Caiaphas. Virgil had never seen this form of punishment in the Inferno before. When he had traveled to the bottom of the Inferno before, Jesus had not yet been crucified.

Virgil then asked one of the Jovial Friars, "Can you tell us, please, how we can leave this pocket without having to call on the black devils who guard the fifth pocket?"

The Jovial Friar replied, "Nearby is a fallen bridge, the ruins of which you may climb up. All of the pockets in this Circle have bridges that cross them, except this one, which has had every bridge smashed."

Virgil was silent for a moment, and then he said, "The black devil named Malacoda lied to me. He said that a bridge across this bolgia is still intact."

The Jovial Friar replied, "I have heard of the devil's many talents, one of which is telling lies."

Virgil quickly walked away, his face contorted with anger.

Dante followed his cherished guide.

Chapter 24: The Thieves, Including Vanni Fucci

When spring is coming but cold days remain, a peasant will sometimes get up early in the morning, look out at the fields, and see what appears to be snow on the ground. Nothing for his sheep to eat! Disappointed, the peasant hits his thighs with his hands. But later, the peasant looks again, and he sees grass. What had appeared to be snow was merely frost. The peasant's brow unfurrows, and he is happy again as he drives his sheep to the grass to eat.

At first Virgil's brow was furrowed as he thought about how he had been tricked by the black devil who had told him that a bridge remained unbroken across the sixth pocket, but as time went on he began to think about how he and Dante had escaped the black devils, and his brow unfurrowed, and he was his usual self again.

Dante and Virgil came to the broken remains of the bridge, and Virgil looked carefully at the ruins, deciding how best to climb them. He then began to climb them, helping Dante to go from rock to rock, and sometimes telling him, "Grab that rock next, but test it to make sure that it will bear your weight."

The climb upward was tough, even though Dante had the help of Virgil and even though Virgil, who was a soul without a body, weighed nothing. This was not a climb for anyone who wore the cloak of the hypocrites! Also fortunately, the bank that they were now climbing was lower than the bank that they had slid down.

Dante thought, *I can't speak for Virgil, but if the bank that we are climbing were as high as the bank that we slid down, I would have given up and stopped climbing.*

They had reached the top, and Dante, severely winded, had to rest and sit down.

"Don't be lazy," Virgil said to him, "Sloth does not result in fame. Sitting on a cushion or lying in bed will not make you famous. Unless you win fame, you will be forgotten. Some kinds of fame are worthwhile and long lasting. If you are slothful, you will be like smoke in the wind or foam upon the water. Stand up, and conquer your laziness! We have another climb — steeper than this! — ahead of us, and we have more sinners to see!"

Dante stood up, pretended to be less winded than he was, and said, "I am ready now. Lead on."

They continued their journey, and they reached and began to cross the next bridge. Dante heard noises, although he could see nothing when he looked down in the pocket, which was shrouded in darkness.

Dante said to Virgil, "Can we go to a point where I see into this bolgia? I can hear sounds, but I cannot see anything."

"Yes, of course," Virgil replied. "Your request is fitting; knowing the punishments in each bolgia is part of your necessary education here."

After they crossed the bridge over this, the seventh bolgia, on the other bank they climbed down to a place where they were able to look down and see into the bolgia. There they saw massive numbers of snakes and lizards and other reptiles, and they saw terrified sinners.

Although the sands of Libya are the home to many reptiles, those sands cannot compare to the seventh bolgia. Many sinners ran in this bolgia among the snakes and lizards. They were terrified and naked. Nowhere was a hiding-place or heliotrope, a stone with the power to cure snakebites and to make its possessor invisible — something that the sinners here wished to be.

Snakes tied the sinners' hands. Snakes wound themselves around the sinners' bodies.

And then a snake struck and bit a sinner, who immediately was consumed by fire and turned to ashes, which then reconstituted themselves into the sinner again. The sinner was dazed, like a person who has suffered and come out of an epileptic fit. The Phoenix will burn into ashes and then be reborn, and so was this sinner.

Virgil asked the sinner, "Who are you? What is your story?"

The sinner replied, "My name is Vanni Fucci, and I have not been in the Inferno very long. I come from Pistoia."

Dante then asked Virgil, "Ask him what is his sin that has put him here. From what I know of him, he was a very angry man and I am surprised that he is not punished in a higher Circle."

The sinner overheard Dante and looked at him, and then said, "I am sorry that you know that I am here. I grieve more for that than I do for my death. But I am here because I am a thief. In 1293, I stole the treasure of San Jacopo. This treasure was located in the Duomo — the cathedral church — of San Zeno.

One of the people falsely accused of the theft spent a year in prison. I, however, avoided paying the penalty for my theft by leaving the area."

Like other sinners here, Vanni Fucci has committed more than one kind of sin, Virgil thought. *He could have been punished in a different Circle, but Minos is a just judge who never errs. Minos sent this sinner to this Circle, and this is where the sinner most deserves to be.*

"I don't want you to feel happy because you have seen me here, so I will make a prophecy for you. Pistoia will lose its Black Guelfs, Florence shall have a change of government, battles and arguments will take place, and the White Guelfs will grieve.

"I have told you this so that you will be unhappy."

Chapter 25: The Transformations of Thieves

After Vanni Fucci had made his prophecy, he formed his hands to make obscene gestures, and then he raised them in the air and shouted, "These are for you, God!"

Dante thought, *Every snake here is my friend because they punish sinners such as Vanni Fucci.*

Good, Virgil thought. *Dante is feeling righteous indignation. He realizes that Vanni Fucci ought to be punished severely.*

A snake immediately coiled itself around Vanni Fucci's neck and stopped him from saying anything more. Another snake bound his arms together in front.

Vanni Fucci's hometown, Pistoia, might as well destroy itself, Dante thought. *Its founders were criminals — the remains of Catiline's army, which tried to end the Roman republic before its time. But its descendants have done more damage than its founders ever did. No sinner I have seen in the Inferno is haughtier than Vanni Fucci — not even Capaneus the blasphemer.*

Unable to speak now, Vanni Fucci fled, and a Centaur appeared. On his back were an enormous number of snakes and a fire-breathing dragon.

Virgil said to Dante, "This Centaur is named Cacus. He is not with the other Centaurs who guard the river of boiling blood because he is a thief. He stole Hercules' cattle and dragged them by the tails into his cave so that their hoof prints would lead in the other direction, away from the cave. One of the cattle lowed, Hercules heard the sound, and he came running to the cave. Cacus barred the doorway, but Hercules tore off the top of the mountain and hurled down boulders to kill Cacus."

Cacus galloped off to find and punish Vanni Fucci, and Dante saw three sinners whom he had not noticed before. They had seen Dante and Virgil first, and they asked, "Who are you?"

Before Dante and Virgil could answer, one of the sinners asked, "Where is Cianfa?"

Dante remained silent, and he motioned for Virgil to also remain silent.

Then they saw something incredible. A six-legged reptile jumped onto a sinner, and the reptile bit both of the sinner's cheeks. The reptile's front legs grabbed the sinner's arms, the reptile's middle legs grabbed the sinner's stomach, and the reptile's rear legs grabbed the sinner's legs. Then the two beings transformed into one being.

The two beings melted and flowed together, and a watching sinner shouted, "Agnèl, you are changing! You are not what you were!"

Transformed into one reptile, the two beings who were now one being walked away.

A small four-legged reptile then bit one of the remaining two thieves. The thief and the four-legged reptile stared at each other, and then they transformed in a way that neither Lucan nor Ovid had ever written about. They wrote about single transformations — one thing turning into another — but what Dante and Virgil now saw was a double transformation: The four-legged reptile transformed into a human thief, and the human thief transformed into a four-legged reptile. The four-legged reptile had stolen the human thief's form.

This is another contrapasso, Virgil thought. *In the living world, the thieves stole things that belonged to other people, and in this bolgia the only thing the naked thieves have — their identity — is stolen by other thieves. The snakes and legged reptiles here are thieves, and the only way for a snake or legged reptile to regain a human form is to steal it from another thief.*

When a snake or legged reptile bites or wraps itself around a thief, one of three things can happen:

One, the thief can be consumed by fire and reduced to ashes, then be refashioned into his own form again (much like the mythical bird known as the Phoenix is consumed by fire, then is reconstituted as a young bird again),

Two, the thief and the snake or legged reptile can unite into one body, or

Three, the thief can become a snake or legged reptile, while the snake or legged reptile becomes a thief with a human form.

Thieves create a lot of uncertainty. You may think that you have something, but you discover that someone has stolen that thing. In a neighborhood where thieves constantly prey, you can never be sure that something you own will stay in your possession. Similarly, the thieves are never sure what will happen when a snake or legged reptile bites a thief.

In addition, the thieves used their limbs to steal from other people and to run away, and now they often become an armless, legless snake.

After regaining his human form, the thief who had been a four-legged reptile said, "Let Buoso have my old form and run on four legs for a while."

I recognize two of the thieves, Dante thought. *One is Puccio Sciencato. Another is Francesco Cavalcanti, aka Guercio. The citizens of Gaville murdered him, and his relatives avenged his death by decimating — killing every 10th man — the population of Gaville.*

Chapter 26: Evil Advisers; Ulysses/Diomedes

Florence, your name is well known in the Inferno, Dante thought. Among the thieves I found five of your most important citizens — and I know that trouble is coming for you.

Now Dante and Virgil climbed up from the vantage point from which they had been able to see into the bolgia of the thieves. Virgil went first, so that he could help pull Dante up the rough spots. In many places, they had to climb while using their hands as well as their feet.

And now they arrived at the eighth bolgia, a place where Dante learned to use his great talents in the service of good, not evil.

Looking into the eighth bolgia, Dante and Virgil saw many, many lights. They looked as numerous as fireflies on a hot summer evening. The lights were flames.

They looked at the flames, which traveled along the bolgia. Dante could not see what was inside the flames, but because he was in the Inferno, he knew that inside the flames were sinners. Similarly, when Elisha witnessed Elijah traveling to Heaven in a fiery chariot, he could see the shining of the chariot in the distance, but not who was in it.

Dante leaned over the bridge so that he could see into the bolgia, and Virgil explained, "Inside the flames are sinners. Burning is part of their punishment."

Dante replied, "I had guessed that already, but I am glad to hear you confirm what I guessed.

"Can you tell who is in the flame whose tip on top is split in two, just like the flame of the pyre on which Eteocles and Polynices, his brother, were burned?"

Eteocles and Polynices were two brothers who agreed to take turns ruling the city of Thebes, Virgil thought. One brother was supposed to rule for a year, then the other brother would rule for a year, and so on. Eteocles ruled for the first year, but then he refused to give up the throne so that his brother could rule for a year. Angry, Polynices gathered an army together and marched against Thebes, creating the story of the Seven Against Thebes. The two brothers killed each other in combat, and when their corpses were cremated together, the flame split in two over their corpses because even in death they were still angry at each other.

"Inside are the souls of Ulysses and Diomedes, two Greek soldiers of the Trojan War," Virgil replied. "Ulysses is also known as Odysseus, which is his Greek name, and Homer wrote in his *Odyssey* about Ulysses' journeys and homecoming after the end of the Trojan War.

"The two warriors are entombed in the flame together because they are angry at each other. Just like Francesca da Rimini and Paolo are together in eternity as part of their punishment, so are Ulysses and Diomedes punished together in eternity.

"Inside the flame Ulysses and Diomedes grieve for three things. The first thing they grieve for is the trick of the Trojan Horse that led to the destruction of Troy and the founding of the Roman people."

I wrote about the trick of the Trojan Horse and the founding of the Roman people in my Aeneid, *Virgil thought. Other epic poets such as Homer also wrote about the Trojan War. Homer's* Iliad *tells the story of events that occur before the Trojan Horse, and Homer's* Odyssey *tells the story of events that occur after the Trojan Horse.*

Ulysses came up with the idea of the Trojan Horse. The Trojan War had been fought for 10 years, and the forces of Agamemnon and the other Greeks had not been able to conquer Troy by might, and so Ulysses had the idea of using trickery to conquer Troy. The Greeks built a huge wooden horse and left it outside Troy, then they seemed to sail away in their ships and return home. However, the Trojan Horse was hollow and filled with Greek soldiers, including Ulysses and Diomedes, and the ships sailed behind an island so that the Trojans could not see them. A lying Greek named Sinon stayed behind and pretended that he had escaped from Ulysses, who had wanted to kill him. Sinon told the Trojans that if the Trojans were to take the Trojan Horse inside the walls of Troy, then Troy would never fall. Amid great rejoicing, the Trojans took the Trojan Horse inside the walls of Troy. That night, the Greek warriors came out of the Trojan Horse, went to the gates of Troy, killed the Trojan guards, and opened the gates of Troy. Agamemnon and his troops were outside the gates, as they had returned from hiding behind the island. The Greeks then conquered Troy, killing many, many Trojans, including Trojan women and children.

After Troy fell, Aeneas led the Trojan survivors to Italy, where the Trojan men married Italian women. Their descendants became the Romans.

"The second thing that they mourn is another trick — the trick that caused Deïdamia to weep over Achilles," Virgil continued.

Both Ulysses and Diomedes were instrumental in making Deïdamia grieve, Virgil thought. *Achilles was the major warrior for the Greeks in the Trojan War, and his mother, the immortal goddess Thetis, knew that he would die at Troy; therefore, she disguised him as a girl and took him to the court of King Lycomedes, where he pretended to be one of the king's daughters. There, he seduced Deïdamia, who bore him a son. Ulysses and Diomedes came to the court of King Lycomedes looking for Achilles, and Ulysses was able to learn his identity through a trick. Ulysses, bringing gifts for the king's daughters, brought a lance and shield with him — Achilles, dressed as a girl, was very interested in those weapons, thus revealing his sex.*

Here Ulysses used his great intellect, but its use had bad consequences: One, Achilles killed many, many Trojans; two, Achilles died; and three, Deïdamia mourned him. This is an example of great but misdirected intellect.

"The third thing that they lament is the theft of the Palladium," Virgil said.

The Palladium was a statue of the goddess Pallas Athena, aka Minerva, Virgil thought. *As long as it remained in Troy, Troy would never fall. Ulysses and Diomedes snuck into Troy one night and carried off the Palladium. Here Ulysses and Diomedes used great daring and probably great intellect, and here once again bad consequences followed. As long as the Palladium stayed in Troy, Troy would not fall. By stealing the Palladium, Ulysses and Diomedes helped cause Troy to fall.*

"Can they speak from within the flame?" Dante asked. "If they can, I would like to know their story."

"You should hear their story," Virgil replied, "But let me do the talking. You and I both are descendants of the Trojans, and for that reason they may not want to speak to us. However, since I am an epic poet and have told part of their stories in my *Aeneid*, that may be enough for one of them to talk to me."

When the flame whose tip was divided in two came near the bridge on which Dante and Virgil were standing, Virgil said, "You — the two souls entombed in one flame — if I have deserved any praise from you while I was living, when I wrote my *Aeneid*, let one of you tell his story. What is your sin, and how did you die?"

The two tips of the flames were of unequal size. The larger of the tips began to move quicker, like a tongue that is talking, and words came out of the flame:

"I am Ulysses, and when Troy fell I journeyed on the seas, and I spent a year with the goddess Circe, who turned my men into swine until I made her turn them back into men.

"I made my way back to Ithaca, but I did not stay there long, even though I had been away for 20 years. I spent 10 years at Troy, and it took an additional 10 years for me to return home to Ithaca. Not the duty I owed to my son, not the duty I owed to my father, not the duty I owed to my loving wife, Penelope, could keep me there. I wanted to seek out more adventures and more knowledge."

Ulysses lacked the Roman virtue of pietas, *Virgil thought. Pietas* is giving *respect where respect is owed: to one's country, to one's father, to one's wife, and to one's son. Ulysses had been away from Ithaca for 20 years, but quickly he grew bored and wanted to set out for adventures, leaving behind his father (Laertes), his wife (Penelope), and his son (Telemachus). These are people who suffered while Ulysses was away from his kingdom of Ithaca, and Ulysses ought to have stayed on Ithaca to take care of his family and his people. Instead, he placed his thirst for adventure ahead of his family and his kingdom. Pietas* is a virtue that Aeneas, the hero of my* Aeneid, *had in abundance.*

"I wanted adventure," Ulysses continued, "and I wanted knowledge and experience — I wanted knowledge and experience of all human vices and of all human virtues."

Part of what you wanted is good, Virgil thought. To want knowledge and experience of all human virtues is a very good thing. But part of what you wanted is very bad. You wanted knowledge and experience of all human vices. That is forbidden knowledge. No one should have the knowledge and experience of being a drug addict, a rapist, a murderer.

"I set sail with a small group of men — not many — who were loyal to me," Ulysses continued. "We sailed the Mediterranean, and we came to the Pillars of Hercules. I wanted to sail beyond them."

The Pillars of Hercules are also known as the Strait of Gibraltar, Virgil thought. Hercules split a mountain in two to form the Pillars of Hercules. This was a warning to pagan sailors not to go any further. Of course, what lies outside the Pillars of Hercules is the Atlantic Ocean, an ocean that was very dangerous for ancient ships to sail on. Any ancient ship that sailed west into the Atlantic Ocean would probably run out of food long before reaching land, and everyone on board would perish. By going beyond the limits set for ancient sailors, Ulysses was seeking forbidden knowledge.

"I was old and tired, and my men were old and tired," Ulysses continued, "but I wanted to sail into the Atlantic Ocean. I told my men, 'Brothers, we have had many adventures together. Let us have another great adventure. Do not deny yourselves anything. Experience everything. We are Greeks, and we were born to pursue knowledge and experience.'"

You scammed your men, Virgil thought. They should have returned to Ithaca, but you convinced them to sail out into the Atlantic Ocean for bad reasons.

"My men cheered, and we set sail into the Atlantic Ocean," Ulysses continued. "Our voyage was mad, but we went. We made our way to the southern hemisphere, and we saw a mountain slope the likes of which I had never seen before. At first, we were happy to see the mountain, but a storm arose from the mountain. The wind crashed into our ship four times, and the fourth time the wind hit our ship, we sank. Above us, the sea grew calm."

I know which mountain you saw, Virgil thought. It was the Mountain of Purgatory, and a pagan must have special permission from God to be on that mountain.

Dante, I hope that you are learning from Ulysses' story. Here we have a man of great abilities, but he did not use his gifts in the correct way. Instead of using his gifts for good, he used them for evil — to seek knowledge and experience of all human vices. You, Dante, have great abilities. Do not misuse them, or you will end up in the Inferno forever.

Chapter 27: Guido da Montefeltro

The flame punishing the souls of Ulysses and Diomedes moved away, and another flame came toward Dante and Virgil, both of whom directed their attention toward this flame because of the roaring sounds that came from its tip.

These roaring sounds remind me of another roar, Virgil thought. Phalaris was a cruel ruler of the city Agrigentum in Sicily. He commissioned Perillus to construct a hollow bull of metal to be used as an instrument of torture. The victim would be placed inside the bull, and then the bull would be heated. As the victim roasted, the victim screamed. Phalaris ordered that the bull be constructed in such a way that the screams of the victims would sound like the bellowing of a bull.

After Perillus used his great abilities to construct the bull — something that he ought not to have done — Phalaris made him the first victim to be placed in the bull and roasted. This is poetic justice, and contrapasso *is very much concerned with poetic justice. Additional poetic justice occurred when Phalaris was overthrown and also became a victim of the bull.*

In this story, we see a person being punished for the misuse of great abilities, and of course, the sinners in this bolgia are being punished for that sin.

I know the story of Guido da Montefeltro, who is like Perillus. He sinned at the request of another person, and he pays for that sin.

The sinner inside the flame had recognized Virgil's dialect and now spoke to him, "It has taken me a while to reach you. Please wait a while and speak to me. If you are a newcomer to Hell, can you tell me news of whether the inhabitants of Romagnol are at war? I come from that region."

Virgil told Dante, "You speak to this sinner — he is Italian."

Dante said to the sinner in the flame, "The leaders of Romagnol always have war in their hearts, but their country is not presently at war, although Romagnol has a troubled past.

"But who are you and what is your story? I did you a favor by answering your question, so do me a favor and answer my question. I can make your fame long-lasting in the Land of the Living."

"If I thought that you would ever leave the Inferno, I would not answer your question," the sinner in the flame answered, "but since I have heard that no one ever leaves here, I will answer your question.

"I am Guido da Montefeltro. I had two careers: First I was a soldier, and then I was a friar. I blame Pope Boniface VIII for my being in Hell. While I was alive, I was wily like a fox. I was shrewd and had great abilities. I was a warrior, but I was also known for trickery. I became world-famous."

Guido is overstating his fame, Virgil thought. *He was important regionally, but he was hardly famous throughout the world.*

"When I grew old, I became concerned about the afterlife," Guido continued. "I confessed my sins, and I became a Franciscan friar — it could have worked!"

It could have worked, you think, Virgil thought, *but obviously it didn't. You are in the Inferno. God does not make mistakes, so you are where you belong. You tried to scam God by becoming a Franciscan* friar, *but obviously it didn't work. Repentant sinners don't end up in the Inferno, so obviously you did not sincerely repent your sins.*

"Pope Boniface VIII chose to make war on a family of Christians instead of making war on the Jews or the Muslims," Guido continued. "Pope Boniface VIII became Pope when Pope Celestine V resigned, but the Colonna family did not believe that the resignation of Pope Celestine V was valid; therefore, the Colonna family opposed Pope Boniface VIII. Pope Boniface VIII ran into a problem. He was fighting the Colonna family, and the Colonna family was barricaded inside Palestrina, a fortified city at the top of a mountain in Italy. Because of the location of the fortified city, it was going to be very, very difficult to take.

"Pope Boniface VIII came to me to give him advice about how to conquer the Colonna family. I stayed silent — Benedictine monks ought to be concerned with peace, not war. They should not give advice about how to conquer Christians.

"Pope Boniface VIII then said to me, 'Don't worry about the fate of your soul. I am the Pope, and I have two keys. These keys will unlock the gates of Heaven. I tell you now that the sin you will commit by answering my question is forgiven.'"

Dante, pay attention, Virgil thought. *Guido da Montefeltro was a scammer while he was alive, but in his story he is now being scammed by Pope Boniface VIII, who is still alive, but who will be damned to Hell when he dies. We know that he will be punished with the other Simonists in the third pocket of Circle 8. Pope Nicholas III, a sinner there, told us that.*

"I was impressed by Pope Boniface VIII's reasoning," Guido continued. "I said to him, 'Father, since you have assured me that my sin is forgiven, this is how you may conquer the Colonna family: Make a promise to them, but do not keep your promise.'"

Guido knew that he was sinning by offering this advice, Virgil thought. *His advice to Pope Boniface VIII was to make promises, and then not keep your promises — tell the Colonna family that you want to be friends and that you will give them what they want, and then when they come out of the fortified city, destroy the city so that the Colonna family no longer has this stronghold. In other words, arrange a truce, and then break the truce as soon as it is advantageous for you.*

In fact, Pope Boniface VIII followed this advice. When the Colonna family left the fortified city, the Pope had it destroyed.

"When I died, Saint Francis came to escort my soul away from Hell," Guido continued, "but one of the black Cherubim also came to get my soul. The fallen angel cried, 'Don't touch this soul! He is mine! Unrepentant sinners go to Hell! He must go down into the Inferno because he did not repent sincerely. A sin cannot be forgiven unless the sinner is repentant, and one cannot repent a sin at the same time that the sinner is committing it! The "repentance" is cancelled out by the deed! Examine my logic for flaws, and you will see that my logic has no flaws.'

"The fallen angel took me to Minos, who wrapped his tail around himself eight times and sent to this place of fire. And here I will stay forever."

Guido spent his life scamming others, yet he did not recognize the scam when Pope Boniface VIII scammed him. He has lost the good of intellect, Virgil thought. *In addition, Guido tried to scam God with a fake repentance. Obviously, that scam failed.*

Ulysses also lost the good of intellect. He should have known that he should have stayed home with his family now that he was old and tired. He should have also realized that it is better not to experience and not to know some things. However, he went on a final voyage and got his men and himself killed.

Dante, we have spent a lot of time in this bolgia because you have something important to learn here. Ulysses and Guido da Montefeltro are very intelligent people. Both felt a temptation to misuse their intelligence and their powers of persuasion. Both scammed other people.

As a very intelligent man, you, Dante, may feel the temptation to misuse your intelligence and your powers of persuasion. Here in the Inferno you need to learn not to do that. If you, Dante, misuse your great abilities, you can end up in the Inferno just like Ulysses, Diomedes, and Guido da Montefeltro.

The flame moved on, and Dante and Virgil continued their journey, moving on to the ninth bolgia, where the sowers of discord are punished.

Chapter 28: The Schismatics

And now Dante and Virgil saw a scene of bloodshed. Imagine the results of many bloody battles with a great number of casualties displaying the horrifying wounds of war: limbs cut off and torsos slit up the middle, and much blood flowing.

One such bloody battle was the Battle of Cannae. During the Second Punic War, the Carthaginian general Hannibal crossed the Alps — with war elephants! — and invaded Italy. He had much early success in the war, although the Romans eventually won. One of Hannibal's greatest successes was at the Battle of Cannae. So many Roman soldiers were killed that the Roman historian Livy related that the Carthaginian soldiers gathered three bushels of gold rings from the fingers of the dead Roman soldiers.

Such blood and carnage as could be seen at Cannae — and other battles — could be seen in the ninth bolgia of Circle 8 of the Inferno. Here the schismatics — the sowers of discord — were punished.

A schism is a break, Virgil thought. *It is especially a break within a church, as in the future will occur between Catholics and Protestants, or as is the case now between the Roman Catholic Church and the Eastern Orthodox Church, or between Islam and Christianity. However, a schism can also occur in politics, as when rival, hate-filled political parties are formed, or within families, as when a son and a father hate each other. In the ninth bolgia, the sowers of religious discord, of political discord, and of familial discord are punished.*

Dante and Virgil saw a sinner whose body was split open from his chin to his anus. His guts had spilled out, and Dante and Virgil could see his heart and his stomach and his intestines.

The sinner looked at Dante, opened up his chest, and said, "Look at how I am punished! I am Mahomet, aka Muhammad, and in front of me is Ali, who weeps. He is split from his chin to the top of the head. The sinners you see here are the schismatics. We walk this Circle, and a devil wielding a sword wounds us. By the time we have completed a round of the Circle, we are healed and the devil wounds us again. Because we caused divisions when we were alive, the devil causes divisions in us now that we are dead."

Muhammad and Ali, the founders of Islam, caused a schism within the Christian Church by having Islam break away from Christianity, Dante thought. *Because of this, these two schismatics are punished by being slit with a sword wielded by a devil.*

Muhammad then asked Dante, "But who are you, and what is your story?"

Virgil answered for Dante, "He is not dead yet, and he has not been sentenced to this bolgia for sins committed in the Land of the Living. I am dead, and I am his guide. My purpose is to educate him by escorting him throughout the Inferno."

Over 100 sinners in the ninth pocket stopped to look at Dante when they heard that he was still alive.

Muhammad said to Dante, "Since you are still alive, when you return to the Land of the Living, tell Fra Dolcino to stock up on food, or else he will lose his struggle and join me here in the Inferno."

Fra Dolcino is a heretic who in 1307 will be burned at the stake, Virgil thought. *Pope Clement V will oppose him, and Fra Dolcino will hide out in some hills near Novaro. He and his followers will run out of food, and the forces of the Pope will be able to capture him and burn him at the stake.*

Another sinner with an ear and his nose cut off, and with his throat cut, said to Dante, "I have seen you when I was alive, unless I am deceived by your resemblance to someone else. If you return to the Land of the Living, remember Pier da Medicina, and tell Messer Guido and Angiolello that they will drown when they are tied in a sack and thrown into the water near Cattolica. A tyrant will murder them."

Dante replied, "If you want me to carry your message back to the Land of the Living, tell me who is the sinner beside you."

Pier da Medicina grabbed the jaws of the sinner beside him and opened them, revealing that the sinner's tongue had been cut out. "This sinner is Curio, whose tongue is cut out each time he completes a journey around the Circle. Curio urged Julius Caesar — who is in Limbo — to cross the Rubicon River, thus starting civil war among the Romans. When Julius Caesar crossed the Rubicon River, he said, 'Thus the die is cast,' meaning that there was no turning back now, as he had disobeyed the orders of the Roman Senate."

Another sinner then showed Dante that his hands had been cut off. He raised the stumps of his blood-dripping arms in the air and said, "I am Mosca, who started the split of Florentines into rival Ghibelline and Guelf factions. Buondelmonte de' Buondelmonti was engaged to be married to the daughter of Lambertuccio degli Amidei, but when a better offer came along — Aldruda, a member of the Donati family, offered him her daughter to be his bride — he took it. Although Aldruda offered to pay the expenses of the broken engagement, this was a major insult to my family, the family of the jilted bride, and I advised that Buondelmonte de' Buondelmonti be killed. After he was killed, the two factions of the Guelfs and the Ghibellines began."

"May all of your family be punished for the evil you have created," Dante, a victim of the schism between the Guelfs and the Ghibellines, said.

Good work, Dante, Virgil thought. *The main thing for you to learn here in this pocket is to recognize the evil of extreme factionalism, and in your reply to Mosca you have shown that you have learned that.*

Dante saw one more thing, a thing so incredible that he wondered whether anyone would believe it. He saw a man whose head had been cut off — the body was carrying the head like a lantern.

The sinner held up his severed head, and the severed head said, "I am Bertran de Born, and in the 12th century I urged Prince Henry of England to rebel against his father, who was King Henry II. Thus, I urged the son of a family to rebel against its head, and so my head is cut off each time I complete a journey around the Circle. My punishment is the perfect *contrapasso*."

Chapter 29: The Falsifiers (Alchemists)

Dante kept looking at the sinners in the ninth bolgia, and Virgil said to him, "Why do you keep staring at these sinners more than you looked at other sinners? This Circle is 22 miles around, and you will not be able to see all the sinners here."

Dante and Virgil moved toward the tenth bolgia, and Dante explained, "I was looking for someone in particular. A member of my family is most likely in that bolgia."

"Think no longer of that member of your family," Virgil replied. "You have other things to think of, and to see. I saw the man you are speaking of. His name is Geri del Bello, and I heard his name called out. You did not see him because you were busy looking at Bertran de Born, but Geri saw you and he was angry."

"I know why he was angry," Dante replied. "He was murdered at the hands of the Sacchetti family, and his murder has not been avenged. Geri del Bello wants me to murder a member of the Sacchetti family to avenge his death."

Yes, Virgil thought, *and if you avenge the death of Geri del Bello by killing a member of the Sacchetti family, then a member of the Sacchetti family will kill either you or a member of your family in retaliation, and the blood feud will continue. In addition, you will most likely end up in the Inferno when you die. I certainly hope that this trip through the Inferno is teaching you to avoid extreme factionalism.*

Now Dante and Virgil reached the bridge over the last of the Malebolge. They looked down, and they saw many sinners who had been afflicted with illness. Imagine all the sick of all the hospitals in a sickness-infested country crammed into one ditch, and you can imagine what Dante and Virgil were seeing.

I have been here before, and I know what kind of sinners are being punished here, and why, Virgil thought. *In the tenth and final bolgia are punished those who are falsifiers of various kinds. These sinners are punished with various illnesses. This is as it should be, for sin is a kind of illness or disease.*

The alchemists have leprosy (the alchemists tried to change lead into gold, and now their skin turns from healthy to diseased). The evil impersonators are insane (the evil impersonators made other people confused about who the evil

All of these sinners are falsifiers. The alchemists are falsifiers of things. The evil impersonators are falsifiers of persons. The counterfeiters are falsifiers of money. The liars are falsifiers of words.

Dante marveled at the numbers of the sinners who were afflicted with illness. Some sinners were lying against or on other sinners. Some sinners crawled on their hands and knees. Many sinners did not have the strength to stand up.

Dante saw two sinners, each leaning against the other's back. They were scratching themselves, trying to kill a never-ending itch. Their skin was covered with scabs, and as they scratched the scabs collected under their fingernails. No curry-comb was ever applied to a horse faster by a stable boy eager for bed than the sinners applied their fingernails to their bodies.

Virgil asked the two sinners, "Are any of the sinners here Italian?"

"Both of us are," answered one of the sinners. "But who are you?"

"I am the guide of this living man," Virgil replied. "My purpose is to show him all the Circles of the Inferno."

Both sinners turned to look at Dante, and Virgil said to Dante, "Ask them whatever you wish."

"So that I may keep your memory from fading away in the Land of the Living," Dante said, "tell me who you are and where you are from."

One of the sinners said, "I am Griffolino da Arezzo, and I told a bishop's son that I could teach him to fly, so that then he could fly through the window of any woman. The bishop's son, whose name was Alberto da Siena, paid me well to teach him how to fly, but of course I could not deliver on my promise; therefore, Alberto reported me to the authorities as a magician, and I was burned at the stake. Of course, this makes me guilty of fraud, but I am punished in the tenth bolgia of Circle 8 of the Inferno for another kind of fraud — that of being an alchemist. Minos sent me here, and Minos cannot err."

Alchemy is a bastard form of chemistry, Virgil thought. *Alchemy is the study of how to turn base metals into gold; for example, an alchemist would love to turn iron, which is cheap, into gold, which is expensive. Alchemists, of course, are guilty of fraud. They get money from other people whom they trick.*

"No people are as silly as the Sienese," Dante said to Virgil.

Capocchio, who had been burned at the stake for alchemy, was the second of the two sinners. Dante had known him when he was alive and they both were students, and then as now Capocchio delighted in mocking the silly Sienese.

Capocchio said to Dante, "Remember the Spendthrifts' Brigade — a club of wealthy Sienese who deliberately wasted their fortunes. One member of the Spendthrifts' Brigade was Niccolo de' Salimbeni. He introduced the use of very expensive cloves to Siena, and he used to set a bed of cloves on fire and roast pheasants over them.

"Dante, if you look closely at me, you will recognize me."

Chapter 30: The Falsifiers (Evil Impersonators, Counterfeiters, and Liars)

The ancient world knew what insanity was.

Juno, the wife of Jupiter, was often jealous, for her husband often gave her good reason to be often jealous. His affairs with other goddesses and with mortal women were many.

When Jupiter had sex with Semele, she bore him the god whose name is Dionysus, aka Bacchus. Juno pretended to become friends with Semele, and she expressed doubt that the father of Semele's child was actually Jupiter. Semele insisted that Jupiter reveal himself to her in his divine form, something that mortals are unable to look upon and live. Her request was insane, and she died, but Jupiter rescued the fetus that was inside her, and he sewed the fetus into his own thigh until the baby was ready to be born. This is why Dionysus is known as "twice-born."

Juno also made insane King Athamas, the husband of Ino, Semele's sister. Ino, the Queen of Thebes, had made Juno angry by raising Dionysus, who was Ino's nephew and Jupiter's son. After Juno drove King Athamas insane, he saw his wife coming toward him with two sons — each of her arms held a son. He thought that she was a lioness and his two sons were lion cubs, and he wanted to kill them. He grabbed one son, whose name was Learchus, and dashed his brain out against a rock. His wife drowned herself and her other son.

Another example of insanity from the ancient world was that of the aged Hecuba, Queen of Troy. For many years, she was happily married to Priam, King of Troy, but Troy was fated to fall, and at the end of her long life, she suffered much misfortune. She saw the great Greek warrior Achilles kill her son Hector, the main defender of Troy. During the fall of Troy, she saw Achilles' son, Neoptolemus, kill her husband, Priam, at the altar of Jupiter. After Troy fell, Hector's son, Astyanax, was thrown from the high walls of Troy and killed. Hecuba and the other women and children of Troy were made slaves. One of her daughters, Polyxena, was sacrificed on the grave of Achilles, and one of her sons, Polydorus, who had been sent away from Troy to Thrace so that the royal bloodline would continue even if Troy were to fall, was murdered for the treasure he had. Hecuba saw the unburied corpse of this son in Thrace. Because the corpse was unburied, her son's soul could not enter the Land of the Dead. To be unable to enter the Land of the Dead is a horrible fate for a soul. All of this suffering took away Hecuba's reason, and she became insane.

Two sinners whom Dante saw in the tenth bolgia of Circle 8 were insane. They were so driven to do acts of horror to the other sinners that no stories of insanity from the ancient world could match what these two sinners in the Inferno did. One insane sinner used his teeth to grab Capocchio by the neck and carry him off.

Griffolino d'Arezzo said, "The insane sinner who grabbed Capocchio by the neck and carried him off was named Gianni Schicchi. He has rabies, and he bites all of us."

Gianni Schicchi is an evil impersonator, Virgil thought. *He had acting ability and he could imitate well the voices of other people, so Simone Donati, the son of a wealthy Florentine patriarch named Buoso Donati, hired him after the patriarch died because he was afraid that the patriarch had left much wealth outside of the family and he wanted Gianni Schicchi to dictate a new will that would leave the wealth to the family. Gianni Schicchi did dictate a new will, but he stated (while pretending to be the dying patriarch) that he wanted a lot of the wealth, including a very valuable mare, to go to Gianni Schicchi.*

"Who is the other insane sinner?" Dante asked Griffolino d'Arezzo.

"She is named Myrrha, and she is another evil impersonator. She fell in love with her own father, pretended to be someone else, and slept with him.

"While they were alive, the evil impersonators made people confused about who they were; now that they are dead, the evil impersonators are insane and are themselves confused about who they are."

Dante then looked at the other sinners in the bolgia. He saw a sinner so afflicted with dropsy, which makes parts of the body swell up, that had his arms and legs been cut off, he would have resembled a lute, a musical instrument that is shaped like a pear. The sinner's belly was enormous, in comparison with which his face was tiny. His mouth was open, in the manner of a person with a raging thirst and parched lips.

"You there," the sinner said, "you who are not being punished here — why, I do not know — look at me and know that my name is Master Adamo. In life, I was rich and I had everything I wanted. In death, I would love to have even one drop of water. In my mind I picture the streams of water in my homeland, and this tortures me even more than my dropsy does.

"In life, I was a counterfeiter. Gold florins are supposed to be made with 24 carats of gold, but the gold florins I made had 21 carats of gold and three carats of a less valuable metal. I would love to see my employers down here in this bolgia with me. If it were possible for me to drag my body even one inch in 100 years, I would have already started on a journey around this Circle to find the one employer who is already supposed to be here and to find the others who will join him. I would have already started on this journey even though this Circle is 11 miles in length and a half-mile, at least, in width.

"As a counterfeiter, I made coins appear to be more valuable than they really were. Now my body is bigger than it should be."

"Who are the two sinners next to you?" Dante asked Master Adamo.

"They were here already when I arrived," Master Adamo replied. "One is Potiphar's wife, who tried to seduce Joseph, who resisted her advances. She then bore false witness against him and said that he had tried to seduce her.

"The other sinner is Sinon, the lying Greek. His lies convinced the Trojans to take the Trojan Horse inside the city of Troy. He convinced the Trojans that if the Trojan Horse were taken inside the city, then Troy would never fall. Of course, he lied. The Trojan Horse was filled with Greek warriors who came out of the horse during the night. They went to the gates of the city, killed the guards, and then opened the gates to let in Agamemnon, leader of the Greek army, and his soldiers. Troy fell that night.

"These liars literally stink so bad in the Inferno because their lies metaphorically stank so bad in the Land of the Living."

Sinon was one of the sinners in the Inferno who did not want his name to be remembered in the Land of the Living. He struck Master Adamo in the belly, which made a sound like a drum being struck. But dropsy had not affected Master Adamo's arms, and he struck Sinon — hard.

The two started wrangling in argument.

Master Adamo said to Sinon, "I may have dropsy, but I still have an arm that is ready to hit you."

Sinon replied, "But your arm was not ready when you were burned at the stake, although it was very ready to engage in counterfeiting."

Master Adamo said, "You are telling the truth now, but you did not tell the truth at Troy."

Sinon replied, "While I was alive, my words were false, and while you were alive, your coins were false. I am in Hell for a few false words, but you are in Hell for many, many false coins."

Master Adamo said, "Remember the Trojan Horse, and may all the world remember the Trojan Horse and the part you played in its story."

Sinon said, "May your punishment continue eternally. May your thirst always be agonizing, and may your body always be swollen."

Master Adamo said, "As much as I suffer, you also suffer. I burn with thirst, and you burn with fever."

Dante kept listening to this vulgar debate, and Virgil was growing bored. Already they had seen enough here. Nothing more was to be learned here, and Dante had much, much more to learn.

"Keep listening to this debate, and I will grow angry," Virgil said to Dante.

Ashamed, Dante turned to Virgil. He was too ashamed to speak, but Virgil knew his thoughts and his repentance.

"You have repented your interest in this useless wrangling between sinners, so let us move on," Virgil said. "We have more to see and more to do. Interest in such petty wrangling as this is useless and silly."

Chapter 31: Towering Giants

Virgil had at first made Dante feel ashamed, but his next words eased Dante's pain, just as Achilles' lance, which he had received from his father, was reputed to injure — and to heal the injury it had caused.

They continued their journey in a place that was not fully day and yet not fully night. Dante was unable to see very far ahead, but he did hear the blast of a horn — a horn that was much louder than thunder. He looked in the direction from which the horn-blast had come, and he remembered the horn of Roland.

Roland was one of the paladins of Charlemagne, Dante thought. *While Roland was leading the rearguard, he and his men were attacked in a pass. Roland was proud and he did not blow his horn for help until it was too late. He and all of his men were killed.*

The sound of the horn that Dante heard now was more ominous than that of the horn of Roland.

Looking ahead, Dante saw what appeared to be towers. He asked Virgil, "What city is this that lies ahead?"

Virgil replied, "You cannot see clearly in this dimness and at this distance. When we reach that place, you will see that you are mistaken that it is a city. But so you are prepared for what you will see, I will tell you that you are seeing giants. They stand in the well that goes from Circle 8 to Circle 9. You are seeing only the top half of their bodies; the rest is in the well, hidden from our sight."

As they approached closer, it was as if a fog had lifted and Dante could now see clearly. A mountain fortress has towers, and here in the Inferno were towering giants, the enemy of Jupiter. Just as the fallen angels had rebelled against their Christian God, so these giants had rebelled against their pagan god. Just as the fallen angels had failed to defeat their Christian God, so the giants had failed to defeat their pagan god.

Jupiter had conquered the giants with his thunderbolts, and now, when the giants heard thunder, they feared.

Dante had approached close enough that he could see clearly the face and features of one of the giants. He could see the head, shoulders, chest, much of the stomach, and the two huge arms of the giant, a member of a race that is now extinct in the Land of the Living.

The giants combined the faculty of intellect with enormous strength and an evil will. No mere mortal man can defeat a being with such a combination of features. Better by far to face criminals who are stupid and weak rather than intelligent and strong.

In Rome is a sculpture of a pine cone that stands over seven feet tall. The face of the giant was just that size. The rest of him was in proportion to the giant's face.

The giant shouted, "*Raphel may amech zabi almi!*"

Contemptuous, Virgil shouted at the giant, "You are a blathering idiot who can shout only nonsense syllables. If you need to make a sound, blow on your horn. It is tied around your neck, and if you weren't so stupid, you could easily find it."

Virgil then said to Dante, "This giant is Nimrod, who was so proud that he thought that he could build a tower that would reach Heaven. To stop the tower from being built, God created many languages instead of the one language that human beings had spoken until that time. Because the workers were now speaking different languages, they were unable to coordinate their actions and so the Tower of Babel was not built. Because of Nimrod's pride, God changed the speech of human beings, and now human beings no longer share the same language.

"We have no need to stay here. He cannot understand our words, just as we cannot understand his nonsense syllables."

Dante and Virgil continued walking, and they came to another giant, who was bigger and fiercer than Nimrod. This giant's arms were bound; one arm was bound in back, and the other arm was bound in front.

"This giant is named Ephialtes," Virgil said to Dante. "He was so proud that he thought that he could overcome Jupiter and the other gods, and so he is chained here. He and his brother — Otus, a twin — attempted to put one mountain on top of another mountain in order to reach the gods and make war on them. The pagan god Apollo killed both brothers."

"If I may, I would like to see Briareus, another giant who challenged Jupiter," Dante said.

"Soon, you will see the giant Antaeus," Virgil said. "Antaeus will be able to help us get down into the final Circle of Hell. He is unchained because when his fellow giants challenged Jupiter, he did not join the fight. Because of that, he is worthy of some respect, although he sinned in other ways.

"Briareus is further away, and we will not be able to see him."

Antaeus, the son of Mother Earth and the sea-god Neptune, was strong as long as he touched his Mother Earth, but he became weak when he was lifted into the air, Virgil thought. He used to challenge passersby, kill them, and collect their skulls hoping to eventually have enough to make a temple to Neptune, his father.

Antaeus fought Hercules. After hurling Antaeus to the ground a number of times, Hercules discovered his secret and lifted him into the air and strangled him.

Ephialtes shook himself, and the earth trembled. Dante felt that he had never come so close to death as he had then.

They reached Antaeus, and Virgil said to him, "You are a great hunter, and you once killed a thousand lions in the valley of Zama, where the Roman general Scipio Africanus defeated the Carthaginian general Hannibal and won the Second Punic War against Carthage.

"You are also strong. Many think that if you had fought alongside the other giants in their war against Jupiter, then the giants would have won.

"Please, if you will, put us down onto Cocytus, the frozen lake of Circle 9. Please don't make us ask one of the other giants, such as Tityus or Typhon, for help. This living man here can give you what you want: fame in the Land of the Living."

Antaeus was willing to help them. He stretched out his hands, and they held Virgil, who told Dante to come to him. Virgil then held Dante as the giant lifted them both.

Dante wished that another way of entering Circle 9 existed, but Antaeus put Virgil and Dante safely down into Circle 9, where are punished the worst sinners who ever existed, including especially Lucifer and Judas.

Antaeus then straightened up, and he was as tall as the mast of a huge ship.

Chapter 32: Caina and Antenora

Here we are at the bottom of the Inferno, Virgil thought. This is where the worst of the worst are punished. The ninth Circle is divided into four rings. Each ring punishes one kind of traitor: traitors against kin/family, traitors against government, traitors against guests, and traitors against benefactors, including God. The traitors are punished by being frozen in ice — being a traitor is a sin committed in cold blood. These are people who have lost all warmth for God and for their fellow human beings. The traitors actively betrayed others, so now they are condemned to perpetual immobility.

In the first ring, Caina, which is named after Cain, who slew Abel, are punished those who were treacherous against kin/family. They are frozen in ice up to their necks. Their heads are looking down, and so they are able to cry.

In the second ring, Antenora, which is named after a Trojan who betrayed his city, are punished those who were treacherous against their countries or political parties. They are frozen in ice up to their necks. Their heads are looking up, and so their tear ducts freeze, and they are unable to cry.

In the third ring, Tolomea, which is named after Ptolemy, a captain of Jericho who murdered his father-in-law and his father-in-law's two sons after inviting them to a feast, are punished those who were treacherous against guests. In this ring, some traitors are completely buried under the ice.

The very bottom of the Inferno is reserved for the very worst sinners of all. In this fourth and final ring of the ninth and final Circle of the Inferno, Judecca, which is named after the apostle Judas, who betrayed Christ, are punished those who were treacherous against their benefactors, and especially God. Lucifer, the angel who led the rebellion against God, is punished here.

A river has been flowing throughout Hell. At various places it has different names. Here it is called Cocytus, which means "Lamentation," and it is a frozen lake. The traitors are frozen in the lake.

Dante looked around, and he wondered whether he would ever be able to find words harsh and grating enough to describe what he saw. To do that, he would need the help of the Muses, who helped Amphion to build the wall around the city of Thebes. They helped him to play the lyre so well that while the music played stones moved on their own and built the wall by themselves.

While Dante was looking at the wall of the well that Antaeus had lowered Virgil and him into, he heard a voice warning him, "Be careful where you walk! Don't kick any of us in the head!"

Dante turned around and saw a frozen lake. In Austria the Danube never freezes as solidly and in Russia the Don never freezes as solidly as did that lake. Like frogs sticking their noses out of water, sinners had their heads sticking out of the ice. The rest of their body was frozen in the ice. Their heads were hanging down so that their tears fell to the ice. This was a luxury because their tears did not freeze their tear ducts shut, and so they were able to continue crying.

Dante looked around, and he saw two sinners frozen together very tightly and very closely. He asked, "Tell me, who are you?"

The two looked at him, and their tears fell and froze, locking them together even more tightly. But their heads were still free, and like goats they butted their heads together, both causing and receiving pain.

Another sinner, nearby, had no ears. They had frozen in the cold, and then they had been broken off by the wind sweeping through this Circle. This sinner said, "Why are you looking at us? If you want to know who these two sinners are, they are Napoleone and Allessandro. They were brothers and rivals in two different political factions: Allessandro was a Guelf, while Napoleone was a Ghibelline. They murdered each other — not because of politics, but over their inheritance.

"These two belong here in Ring #1 of Circle 9, which is called Caina and which punishes those who were traitors to kin and family. No one deserves to be here more. Not even Mordred deserves to be here more.

"Mordred was the nephew of King Arthur of Camelot, but he was a traitor to the King, his uncle. In their final battle, nearly everyone was dead. King Arthur charged at Mordred and killed him, but Mordred mortally wounded King Arthur. When King Arthur stabbed Mordred with a spear, the hole created in Mordred was so big that the Sun shone through it, putting a hole in his shadow. Merlin the magician caused King Arthur to fall into a trance and then Merlin hid him in a cave.

"Mordred's greed for power — along with Sir Lancelot's adulterous relationship with King Arthur's Queen — helped to destroy a civilization. King Arthur had instituted a great civilization, but after the civil war started that was caused by Sir Lancelot's adulterous relationship with King Arthur's Queen and by Sir Mordred's greed for power, England's civilization was destroyed and England slipped back into a Dark Age.

"My name is Camicion de' Pazzi, and I murdered a relative named Ubertino. I tell you my name so that I may name Carlin, whose guilt will make my own guilt seem less. Carlin is Carlino de' Pazzi, who, in July of 1302, will surrender a castle to the Black Guelfs of Florence after accepting a bribe, even though his job is to defend the castle for the White Guelfs of Florence. Carlin will be a traitor to country and so will be punished in Antenora, a lower place in Hell than the place that punishes me."

Dante looked around, and he saw over 1,000 sinners frozen in the ice. After he returned to the Land of the Living, he was never able to look at a frozen pond without shuddering.

As Dante and Virgil continued their journey, Dante kicked — hard — one of the heads protruding out of the frozen lake. Perhaps the kick was accidental, but perhaps not.

"Why did you kick me?" the sinner screamed. "Have you come to take revenge on me for what I did at the Battle of Montaperti?"

Dante said to Virgil, "Please wait a little while. I want to talk to this sinner so that I may understand something."

Then Dante said to the sinner, "Who are you to be shouting at other people?"

The sinner replied, "And who are you to be walking through Antenora, Ring #2 of Circle 9, which punishes those who were traitors to their countries or political parties? Who are you to kick sinners in the face? No living man could kick as hard as you!"

"I am still a living man," Dante said. "Speak to me if you want to be remembered in the Land of the Living."

"I definitely do NOT want to be remembered in the Land of the Living," the sinner replied. "Better by far for my name to be quickly forgotten."

Dante grabbed the sinner's hair and threatened, "Tell me your name, or I will not leave even one hair on your head."

"Tear all my hair out," the sinner replied. "I will never tell you my name."

Dante did exactly as he had threatened, tearing out handfuls of the sinner's hair while the sinner yelped.

A nearby sinner said, "What's wrong, Bocca? Usually, I hear your chattering teeth; it's even worse to hear your yelping."

"I know your name now, traitor," Dante said. "I will make sure that your name continues to be known in the Land of the Living and that everybody knows your sin."

Indeed I will, Dante thought. This sinner is Bocca, and he was a traitor to his city. In 1260, at the Battle of Montaperti, in which Farinata, the heretic punished in Circle 6, was one of the generals of the troops fighting against Florence, Farinata's troops were outnumbered. However, Farinata had a secret trick. He had Bocca on his side. Bocca supposedly was on the side of the Guelfs in the battle, but during the fighting he cut off the hand of the man bearing the Florentine standard. The standard fell, and this led to confusion among the Guelfs, who thought that their generals had been captured. This confusion led to the Ghibellines defeating the Guelfs.

"Get out of here!" Bocca yelled. "But since you are going to tell the world about me, be sure that you tell the world about the sinner who revealed my name to you. He is the traitor Buoso da Duera, and he accepted a bribe from Charles of Anjou, who marched against Naples in 1265. Although Buoso da Duera was supposed to lead troops against Charles of Anjou, he allowed him and his troops to pass by without having to fight.

"Other famous traitors are punished here, too. Ganelon, who betrayed Roland and forced him to sound his horn — too late — is here."

Dante and Virgil continued on their journey, and they came to two figures frozen in the ice. One sinner's head was above the other sinner's head, and this sinner was eating the other sinner's head, sinking his teeth into the neck and scalp and chewing.

Dante said to the sinner who was cannibalizing the other sinner, "Tell me your story. Why are you doing this? What is the reason? If you tell me, I can make the reason known in the Land of the Living."

Chapter 33: Tolomea (Ugolino and Ruggieri)

I know the story of these two sinners, Virgil thought. *They are Ugolino and Ruggieri. Ugolino is Ugolino della Gherardesca, the Count of Donortico, and he is a Ghibelline. Ruggieri is Archbishop Ruggieri degli Ubaldini, and he is a Guelf. Their story took place in Pisa, a Ghibelline city that is surrounded by Guelf cities. Often, the Guelf cities tried to take control over things such as castles in Pisan territory.*

The Archbishop of Pisa, Ruggieri, a Ghibelline, decided that it would be a good idea to hire a Guelf as city manager, aka podesta. *Since the city manager would be a Guelf, he would be able to make better deals with the Guelfs; after all, they would be from the same party. Therefore, Ugolino was hired to be* podesta *of Pisa.*

Immediately, Ugolino and Ruggieri began jockeying for power. Ugolino betrayed Pisa by giving good deals to Guelf cities, even giving them castles. Ruggieri was worried because now he had to share power with Ugolino. They worked against each other.

Ruggieri locked Ugolino and his progeny in a tower and starved them to death.

Ugolino and Ruggieri are actually in two different rings in Circle 9. Ugolino betrayed Pisa by giving good deals and good castles to Pisa's Guelf enemies; therefore, he is a traitor to country and is punished in Ring #2: Antenora. Ruggieri betrayed Ugolino by locking him and his progeny in a tower and starving them to death; therefore, he is a traitor to guests or associates and is punished in Ring #3: Tolomea.

The sinner who was cannibalizing the head of the other sinner wiped his bloody mouth on the other sinner and then said, "You want me to tell a story that will cause me grief, but I am willing to tell it so that this sinner's deeds will be known and remembered.

"Know that I am Count Ugolino, and the head I am biting belongs to Archbishop Ruggieri. You probably know much of my story already — but not the heartbreaking details.

"I trusted Archbishop Ruggieri, and because I trusted him, my children and I ended up in prison. Listen, and you shall learn why I make his head my never-ending meal!

"In the tower where we were imprisoned was a window that consisted of a narrow slit. Through it I saw the moon wax and wane many times until one night I had a dream that revealed our evil future.

"I dreamed that Archbishop Ruggieri was a hunter, and he was hunting a father wolf and his wolf cubs. The hunting dogs found the weary father wolf and his wolf cubs and ripped them to pieces.

"When I woke up, I heard my children, still asleep, crying out in their dreams for food.

"If you do not cry at what I am telling you, do you ever cry?

"My children awoke, and I heard nails being pounded into the door through which our food was pushed. I knew then that we would die of starvation. I did not weep, for inside I was stone.

"My children wept, and Anselmuccio said to me, 'What is wrong, father?'

"I did not cry. We were not fed. As days passed by without food, in anguish I bit my hands.

"My children thought that I was biting my hands because of hunger, and they said, 'Feed upon us, father. You gave us our flesh; now take our flesh from us!'

"On the fourth day without food, my Gaddo fell to the floor, crying, 'Help me, father!' Then he died.

"My other three children died in the following days, and for two days I called their names. Then I learned which is more powerful: grief or hunger."

And then you ate the flesh of your children, Virgil thought. *But like other sinners in the Inferno, you have told a self-serving story. Both you and Archbishop Ruggieri are unrepentant sinners, as we know from the fact that both of you are in the Inferno. Both of you betrayed the other. Both of you did some pretty nasty things to each other. You have told us the nasty things that Archbishop Ruggieri did to you, but you have left out the nasty things that you did to Archbishop Ruggieri.*

"Also, you have been misleading in your story. You make it sound as if the four members of your family were all very young sons of yours. Actually, you were imprisoned with two sons and two grandsons. Three were adults; only one was a minor of 15 years old. Still, they were innocent, while you were guilty. Extreme factionalism results in the death of innocents.

Your punishment in the Inferno is fitting. This punishment reenacts your final act on Earth: eating the flesh of your children and grandchildren. You are condemned to reenact this forever.

Ruggieri, of course, placed you in a position where you were so hungry that you starved to death, so it is fitting that he is the object of your cannibalism here.

You, Ugolino, are getting what you want here: You want to eat Ruggieri's flesh, and you are doing exactly that.

And Ugolino, you asked Dante, "If you do not cry at what I am telling you, do you ever cry?" But then you said that you did not cry. Why not? You are an evil man. You have been involved in devious political manipulations and betrayals. At this point, your heart has turned to stone. In the future, the King James Version translation of Ezekiel 36:26 will say, "A new heart also will I give you, and a new spirit will I put within you: and I will take away the stony heart out of your flesh, and I will give you an heart of flesh."

You, Ugolino, have not done the things that would earn you a heart of flesh. You have done, however, the kind of things that have earned you a heart of stone.

You two sinners have engaged in extreme factionalism. You two sinners have gotten innocents killed. You two sinners have not had the proper relationship between church and state government.

Having finished speaking, Ugolino returned to his meal, and Dante and Virgil walked on. Dante mourned the death of the innocents, but he did not mourn the punishment of Ugolino and Ruggieri, who were two very evil sinners.

Dante noticed the wind now, and he asked Virgil what was its cause. Virgil replied, "You will soon see for yourself what is causing this wind."

In Ring #3, which is named Tolomea, the faces looked up rather than down. The icy tears of the sinners froze their tear ducts, denying them the luxury of crying more tears.

A sinner frozen in the ice saw Dante and Virgil and thought that they were sinners destined for the final ring of the final Circle of the Inferno. The sinner called out, "Oh, wicked souls who are so evil that you have been sentenced to that part of the Inferno that punishes the very worst sinners, break the frozen tears off my eyes so that I may cry some more until the new tears freeze."

"Tell me your name, and I will either do what you request or go beneath this ice," Dante replied.

You, Dante, are torturing this sinner, Virgil thought, *and this sinner deserves to be tortured. You, Dante, may know that you will go beneath this ice because you know that we are going downward. Once we reach the very center of the Earth, we must climb upward to the other side of the world, and to do that we must go underneath this ice.*

The sinner replied, "I am Friar Alberigo, and I betrayed my guests. I invited a close relative named Manfred and Manfred's son to supper, and then I had them murdered. I called for fruit to be served, and 'Bring in the fruit' was the prearranged signal for my men to murder my guests. However, I am being punished worse than I deserve."

No, you are being punished exactly as much as you deserve, Virgil thought. *God does not make mistakes. You are not actually dead yet, for your body will die in 1307, and the year now is 1300. But since you are here before you are dead, you deserve to be here.*

"I am surprised to hear your name," Dante said. "I thought that you were still alive."

"This section of Tolomea is special," Friar Alberigo replied. "Some sinners here were so evil that their souls came here before their body died. In the Land of the Living, a demon is inside my body, doing with it I don't know what.

"Other sinners here are in the same fix. Another sinner who has sinned so badly that his soul ended up in the Inferno while a demon inhabits his body until the body's death is Ser Branca D'Oria. A third sinner in the same situation is a close kinsman of Ser Branca who helped him commit his crime: Ser Branca invited his father-in-law, Michel Zanche, to dine with him, and then murdered him."

"That can't be right," Dante said. "Branca D'Oria is still alive, eating and drinking and sleeping."

"It is as I have told you," Friar Alberigo replied. "The soul of Branca D'Oria is here, while a demon inhabits his body in the Land of the Living.

"But do as you promised and break the frozen tears from my face so that I may cry some more."

Dante ignored the request. Friar Alberigo was a sinner. He did not deserve even to cry.

Dante thought, *How sinful men can be. They can be so sinful that their souls are already in Hell although their bodies seem to be alive on Earth.*

Chapter 34: The Ultimate Evil

Virgil said to Dante, "*Vexilla regis prodeunt Inferni*," which means, "The banners of the king of the Inferno advance."

Dante looked, and he saw what seemed to be a huge windmill in the distance. Coming from it were gusts of wind. When he would get closer, he would see that this was not a windmill, but instead the worst sinner of all time: Lucifer, the angel who rebelled against God. Creating the wind were the flapping bat-like wings of Lucifer. The more he flapped his wings in his attempt to escape from the ice, the harder the wind from his wings froze the ice, making his escape even more impossible.

Dante looked down, and he saw that now the sinners were completely encased in the ice in grotesque positions. Some lay flat. Some stood erect. Some were frozen in the ice standing on their heads. Some were frozen bent in the middle, with their heads near their feet.

Dante and Virgil kept walking, and Virgil said, "This is the worst sinner of all time. His name is Dis. His name is Lucifer. His name is Satan. Looking at him up close will take all the courage you have."

Dante looked, and he saw that Lucifer was frozen in the ice up to the midpoint of his chest. Lucifer was once the most beautiful of all of the angels, but Dante saw that Lucifer was now the foulest of all beings. Lucifer had one head, but he had three faces — a perversion of the Holy Trinity. The face in the middle was red, the color of anger. The face on the right was white blended with yellow, the color of impotence. The face on the left was black, the color of ignorance.

Beneath each face were two wings like those of bats. Lucifer continually flapped his three sets of wings, keeping three winds howling in Circle 9 and keeping the lake frozen solid. Each face had two eyes, which continually cried. Each face had a mouth, and each mouth chewed on a sinner. Here were the three worst human sinners of all time.

"The sinner is the middle, whose feet are sticking out of Lucifer's mouth, is the worst human sinner of all time: Judas, who betrayed the Son of God," Virgil said. "The other two sinners, whose top halves are sticking out of Lucifer's other mouths, are Cassius and Brutus."

Cassius and Brutus are the second and third worst human sinners of all time, Virgil thought. *God supported the formation of the Roman Empire and so the Roman Empire was divinely willed. The Roman Empire was known for its rule of law, and for its peace — the* Pax Romana. *By opposing the formation of the Roman Empire through their assassination of Julius Caesar, Brutus and Cassius were traitors to God. Thus, Brutus and Cassius were traitors to their benefactors, both spiritual and temporal. Also, by assassinating Julius Caesar, they ensured that more power struggles would come into existence and more people would be killed before the Roman Empire came into existence.*

Virgil then said to Dante, "You have now seen all of the Inferno, so it is time for us to leave. Hold on to my neck, and I will carry you."

As Virgil had asked him to, Dante held on to his neck, and Virgil climbed down Lucifer's body, holding on the hair on Lucifer's side and thigh. When he reached the midpoint of Lucifer's body, where the thigh begins, Virgil turned and suddenly and surprisingly Dante felt that now they were moving upward. He thought at first that Virgil was climbing back toward Lucifer's head but then he saw Lucifer's legs rising upward. The sight reminded him of the simonists' legs sticking out of the flaming holes that they had landed in.

Panting from the effort, Virgil said to Dante, "This is the only way that we can get to where we now need to go. A moment ago it was night; now it is day."

They reached a cavern and rested. Dante asked Virgil to explain what had happened.

Virgil said, "We reached the center of the Earth when we reached Lucifer's midpoint. We went from one side of the Earth to the other side and so night became day, and so instead of climbing down we began to climb up."

Many of the sinners in the Inferno believe themselves to be the center of the universe, Virgil thought. *Well, what is at the center of the universe? I know. It is Lucifer's crotch. The exact center of the universe is that place where food is not food anymore.*

"Now we are in the Southern Hemisphere, which is completely covered by water except for the Mountain of Purgatory," Virgil continued. "When Lucifer was thrown out of Heaven, he fell to Earth directly opposite Jerusalem. All of the land rushed away from him in fear, some of it creating the Mountain of Purgatory, where we are going next, and some of it fleeing to the Northern Hemisphere.

"We now must climb upward. There is a passage in the rock through which a stream flows. The stream is Lethe, from which saved souls drink after they have climbed the Mountain of Purgatory. Drinking from Lethe causes the saved souls to stop hurting from sin, although they remember that they have sinned and are grateful that God has forgiven them for their sins. The Inferno draws evil and sin and hurt to itself, so the stream — and the hurt of the sin — flows here."

Dante and Virgil climbed upward, and they reached the surface of the earth again. The climb took a long time, and when they reached the surface, Dante saw that it was now night in the Southern Hemisphere. It was just before Easter Sunday, April 10, 1300. Dante looked up and saw the stars.

Background Information

• Who was Dante Alighieri?

Dante, of course, is the author of *The Divine Comedy*. He was born a Roman Catholic in Florence in 1265 C.E. He died of malaria in Ravenna, Italy, in 1321 (the night of Sept. 13-14). He remains buried in Ravenna, although an empty tomb in Florence is dedicated to him. Dante is known for his ability as a world-class poet, for his interest in politics, and for being exiled from Florence. In a way, he remains exiled from Florence, as his body is not in a tomb in Florence.

• What is *The Divine Comedy* in essence?

The Divine Comedy tells about Dante's imaginative journey through the afterlife. Dante finds himself in a dark wood of error, and his guide, Virgil, the author of the Roman epic the *Aeneid*, takes Dante through the Inferno (Hell), and up the Mountain of Purgatory to the Forest of Eden. There Beatrice, Dante's beloved who died early in life, takes over as Dante's guide, and the two ascend the spheres of Paradise, until finally Dante, with the aid of another guide and of the Virgin Mary, is able to see God face to face. These three parts of Dante's imaginative journey make up the three parts of *The Divine Comedy*: the *Inferno*, the *Purgatory*, and the *Paradise*.

In *The Divine Comedy*, Dante tells the reader how to achieve Paradise. In addition, the epic is a love story. A woman saves Dante.

• How long does the journey in *The Divine Comedy* take?

Considering all the distance that is traveled, it doesn't take long at all. It begins on the night before Good Friday and ends on Easter Wednesday of the year 1300, when Dante was 35 years old (midway through his three score and ten years). The journey takes roughly five and a half days. The year 1300 is significant other than being the midpoint of Dante's life. In 1300, spiritual repentance and spiritual renewal were major themes of the Catholic Church's first Holy Year.

• What is the scope of *The Divine Comedy*?

Herman Melville, author of *Moby Dick*, once said that in order to write a mighty book, an author needs to choose a mighty theme. By choosing the afterlife as his theme, Dante chose a mighty theme. He writes about the Inferno and how sins are punished, about Purgatory and how sins are purged, and about Paradise and how good souls are rewarded. In doing this, he writes about many themes that are important to people of his time and to people of our time and to people of any time: religion, God, poetry, politics, etc.

- **Is *The Divine Comedy* universal?**

"Universal" means applicable to anyone, at any time, and anywhere. Yes, *The Divine Comedy* is universal. One need not be a Christian to enjoy and learn from *The Divine Comedy*. All of us sin, and probably most of us regret sinning. Many people can identify with the characters of *The Divine Comedy*. For example, Francesca da Rimini refuses to take responsibility for her actions, instead casting blame on other people. Many of us have done exactly the same thing.

Reading *The Divine Comedy* seriously will take some work. Readers will need to know something about Dante's biography, about the history of his time and previous eras, and about literature. However, *The Divine Comedy* is relevant to our lives today, and this book and its companion volumes can be your guide to Dante's *Divine Comedy*.

- **What are some of the really big issues that are of concern to *The Divine Comedy*?**

One big issue is sin. For example, what are the results of sin?

One big issue is spiritual transformation. For example, how can one purge him- or herself of sin?

One big issue is politics. For example, Dante warns the reader about the dangers of extreme factionalism.

One big issue is poetry. How can poetry help us?

Of course, one really big issue is this: How do I enter Paradise?

- **This book can be your guide to *The Inferno*. What is the purpose of a guide?**

A guide will help you to cover territory safely the first time you go through the territory. However, many guides, including teachers, want to make themselves irrelevant. By reading this book as you read Dante's *Inferno*, you will get a good grasp of the material, but I hope that you continue to read *The Divine Comedy* and the *Inferno* on your own, making it a part of your life and going beyond what is written here. *The Divine Comedy* is one of the Great

Books of Western Literature — a book that you can reread with interest and profit each year of your life.

• Briefly, what are the major facts of the biography of Dante the Poet?

Dante was born in 1265 in Florence, Italy. He was successful in both poetry and politics. Early, he fell in love with Beatrice, a woman who died young in 1290. Both Dante and Beatrice married other people. About Beatrice Dante wrote a group of poems that he published in a volume (with commentary) titled *Vita Nuova* (*The New Life*).

Dante was a member of the political group known as the Guelfs, but when the Guelfs split into rival factions, he became a White Guelf. The White Guelfs opposed the Pope and wanted Florence to be free from papal power, while the Black Guelfs supported the Pope and were willing to do his bidding if he put them in power. Not surprisingly, Pope Boniface VIII supported the Black Guelfs, and he sent troops to Florence who took over the city in November of 1301. We can date Dante's exile from Florence at this time, but he was officially exiled in January of 1302. Dante never returned to Florence.

While in exile, Dante composed his masterpiece: *The Divine Comedy*. He died on Ravenna in 1321 at age 56.

By the way, "Guelf" is sometimes spelled "Guelph."

• What does the title *The Divine Comedy* mean?

Dante called his poem the *Commedia* or *Comedy*. In the 16th century, the word *Divina* or *Divine* was added to the title to show that it was a work rooted in religion.

The Divine Comedy is a "comedy" for two reasons:

1) *The Divine Comedy* was not written in Latin, but was instead written in the "vulgar" language of Italian. Being written in a "vulgar" language, the vernacular, it is written in a language that was regarded as not suited for tragedy.

2) The epic poem has a happy ending.

• What is the difference between Dante the Pilgrim and Dante the Poet?

Dante the Pilgrim is different from Dante the Poet. Dante the Pilgrim is a character in *The Divine Comedy*. At the beginning, he is naive and sometimes believes the spin that the sinners in the *Inferno* put on their own stories. However, Dante the Poet is an older, wiser Dante. Dante the Poet has journeyed throughout the Inferno, Purgatory, and Paradise, and he sees through the stories that the sinners tell in the *Inferno*.

Dante the Poet is the author of *The Divine Comedy*, whose major character is Dante the Pilgrim. Dante the Poet has more knowledge and experience than Dante the Pilgrim.

For example, Dante the Poet knows that he has been exiled from Florence because he is in exile when he writes *The Divine Comedy*. Because the poem is set in 1300, and Dante is not officially exiled until 1302, Dante the Pilgrim does not know at the beginning of the poem that he will be exiled. He will hear the prophecies of his upcoming exile that are made in the *Inferno*, but he will not fully understand that he will be exiled until his ancestor, Cacciaguida, clearly tells him that in the *Paradise*.

Dante the Poet is also more intelligent than Dante the Pilgrim. Dante the Pilgrim will sometimes be taken in by the spin that sinners in the *Inferno* put on their stories, but Dante the Poet knows that God does not make mistakes. If a sinner is in the Inferno, Dante the Poet knows that the sinner belongs there.

- ***The Divine Comedy* is an allegory. Define "allegory."**

An allegory has a double meaning. It can be understood on a literal level, but also present is a symbolic level. Literally, Dante the Pilgrim travels through the Inferno, Purgatory, and Paradise. Symbolically, a human soul who will be saved faces trials, overcomes them, and achieves Paradise.

Allegories have many symbols.

- **What do you need to be in the Afterlife in Dante's Inferno?**

You must meet three criteria:

1) You must be dead.

2) You must be dead in 1300 (with a few exceptions where a soul is in the Inferno while a demon occupies the soul's body in the living world).

3) You must be a dead unrepentant sinner. (After all, if you were a dead repentant sinner, you would be found in either Purgatory or Paradise.)

- **What does it mean to repent?**

To repent your sins means to regret them. Of course, this does not mean regretting being caught for doing them, but regretting the sins themselves.

The sinners Dante will meet in the Inferno are unrepentant sinners. The repentant sinners he will meet in Purgatory treat Dante very much differently from the way the unrepentant sinners he meets in the Inferno treat him.

• **What is the geography of Hell? In *The Divine Comedy*, where is Hell located?**

Dante did not think that the world was flat. (Educated people of his time did not think the world was flat.) To get to the Inferno, you go down. The story is that Lucifer rebelled against God, was thrown from Paradise to the Earth, and landed on the point of the earth that is opposite to Jerusalem. His landing made the Southern Hemisphere composed of water as the land rushed under the water to hide from him. In addition, when he fell to the center of the Earth the land he displaced formed the Mountain of Purgatory.

Dante and Virgil will climb down to the center of the Earth, where Lucifer is punished, then they will keep climbing up to the other side of the world, where they will climb Mount Purgatory.

• **Explain the three separate kinds of moral failure: incontinence, violence, and fraud.**

Incontinence

Incontinence is not being able to control yourself. For example, you may not be able to control your sexual desire (lust) or your desire for food and drink (gluttony).

Violence

Violence can be directed against yourself (suicide), against God (blasphemy), or against other people (physical violence).

Fraud

Fraud involves the willful use of misrepresentation to deprive another person of his or her rights. For example, one can claim to be able to foretell the future and charge people money to tell them their "futures."

Simple fraud is fraud, but it is not committed against those to whom one has a special obligation of trust.

Complex fraud is fraud committed against those to whom one has a special obligation of trust. Sinners who commit complex fraud are traitors of various kinds: e.g., traitors to kin/family, traitors to government, traitors to guests, or traitors to God.

• **What kinds of characters will we see in *The Divine Comedy*?**

We will see both real characters and fictional characters. Mythological creatures will often be the guards in the Inferno.

Some of the characters will be important historically and globally, while others will be important only locally and would in fact be forgotten if they had not been mentioned in the *Inferno*.

• What do the sinners in the Inferno all have in common? Why can't we take what the sinners say at face value?

They have in common the fact that they are unrepentant. They do not take responsibility for the sins they have committed. Because of that, they will spin their stories and try to put the blame on someone or something else.

When we read the *Inferno*, we must be careful to try to see the whole story. The sinners will **not** tell the truth, the whole truth, and nothing but the truth. (Reading this retelling of Dante's *Inferno* or the notes in the translation of the *Inferno* that you are reading can help you to understand when a character is trying to spin you.)

Be aware that many people in the *Inferno* are going to be able to tell a good story, and you may end up thinking — like Dante the Pilgrim sometimes — that a certain sinner does not belong in Hell. However, Dante the Poet realizes that God doesn't make mistakes. Anyone who is in Hell deserves to be in Hell. It's important to closely examine the stories of some persuasive sinners to see what they are leaving out.

• Why do people sin?

Two main reasons, perhaps:

1) A lack of will. Often, we know what we ought to do, but we can't bring ourselves to do it. (Everyone who needs to lose 10 pounds knows exactly what to do to lose it: Exercise more and eat less. Someone who exercises less than they should and eats more than they should without a good reason such as illness is guilty of the sin of gluttony.)

2) An attractive veneer. Sometimes, sinning can appear to be attractive and to be fun, and thus people are tempted to sin. (Staying up late, getting drunk, and partying can be fun, but if these things prevent a student from attending class, that student is guilty of the sin of sloth.)

• Does God make mistakes? Do these sinners belong in the Inferno?

We must be careful when reading the *Inferno*. Dante the Pilgrim will sympathize with some sinners early in the *Inferno*, and we may be tempted to do exactly the same thing, but God is omniscient, omnipotent, and omnibenevolent. God does not make mistakes. If a sinner is in the Inferno, the sinner belongs there.

By the way, the difference between *Inferno* and Inferno is that *Inferno* is the title of a book and Inferno is the name of a place. (Similarly, *Hamlet* is the title of a play, and Hamlet is the name of a character in that play.)

Conclusion

Once you have read this retelling in prose of Dante's great epic poem *Inferno*, you will have a good but basic understanding of it.

Then go and read the real thing. I recommend the translation by Mark Musa. The translation by John Ciardi is also very good.

About the Author

It was a dark and stormy night. Suddenly a cry rang out, and on a hot summer night in 1954, Josephine, wife of Carl Bruce, gave birth to a boy — me. Unfortunately, this young married couple allowed Reuben Saturday, Josephine's brother, to name their first-born. Reuben, aka "The Joker," decided that Bruce was a nice name, so he decided to name me Bruce Bruce. I have gone by my middle name — David — ever since.

Being named Bruce David Bruce hasn't been all bad. Bank tellers remember me very quickly, so I don't often have to show an ID. It can be fun in charades, also. When I was a counselor as a teenager at Camp Echoing Hills in Warsaw, Ohio, a fellow counselor gave the signs for "sounds like" and "two words," then she pointed to a bruise on her leg twice. Bruise Bruise? Oh yeah, Bruce Bruce is the answer!

Uncle Reuben, by the way, gave me a haircut when I was in kindergarten. He cut my hair short and shaved a small bald spot on the back of my head. My mother wouldn't let me go to school until the bald spot grew out again.

Of all my brothers and sisters (six in all), I am the only transplant to Athens, Ohio. I was born in Newark, Ohio, and have lived all around Southeastern Ohio. However, I moved to Athens to go to Ohio University and have never left.

At Ohio U, I never could make up my mind whether to major in English or Philosophy, so I got a bachelor's degree with a double major in both areas, then I added a Master of Arts degree in English and a Master of Arts degree in Philosophy. Yes, I have my MAMA degree.

Currently, and for a long time to come (I eat fruits and veggies), I am spending my retirement writing books such as *Nadia Comaneci: Perfect 10*, *The Funniest People in Comedy*, *Homer's* Iliad: *A Retelling in Prose*, and *William Shakespeare's* Hamlet: *A Retelling in Prose*.

If all goes well, I will publish one or two books a year for the rest of my life. (On the other hand, a good way to make God laugh is to tell Her your plans.)

By the way, my sister Brenda Kennedy writes romances such as *A New Beginning* and *Shattered Dreams*.

Some Books by David Bruce

Retellings of a Classic Work of Literature

Ben Jonson's The Alchemist: *A Retelling*

Ben Jonson's The Arraignment, or Poetaster: *A Retelling*

Ben Jonson's Bartholomew Fair: *A Retelling*

Ben Jonson's The Case is Altered: *A Retelling*

Ben Jonson's Catiline's Conspiracy: *A Retelling*

Ben Jonson's The Devil is an Ass: *A Retelling*

Ben Jonson's Epicene: *A Retelling*

Ben Jonson's Every Man in His Humor: *A Retelling*

Ben Jonson's Every Man Out of His Humor: *A Retelling*

Ben Jonson's The Fountain of Self-Love, or Cynthia's Revels: *A Retelling*

Ben Jonson's The Magnetic Lady, or Humors Reconciled: *A Retelling*

Ben Jonson's The New Inn, or The Light Heart: *A Retelling*

Ben Jonson's Sejanus' Fall: *A Retelling*

Ben Jonson's The Staple of News: *A Retelling*

Ben Jonson's A Tale of a Tub: *A Retelling*

Ben Jonson's Volpone, or the Fox: *A Retelling*

Christopher Marlowe's Complete Plays: Retellings

Christopher Marlowe's Dido, Queen of Carthage: *A Retelling*

Christopher Marlowe's Doctor Faustus: *Retellings of the 1604 A-Text and of the 1616 B-Text*

Christopher Marlowe's Edward II: *A Retelling*

The Trojan War and Its Aftermath: Four Ancient Epic Poems

Virgil's Aeneid: *A Retelling in Prose*

William Shakespeare's 5 Late Romances: Retellings in Prose

William Shakespeare's 10 Histories: Retellings in Prose

William Shakespeare's 11 Tragedies: Retellings in Prose

William Shakespeare's 12 Comedies: Retellings in Prose

William Shakespeare's 38 Plays: Retellings in Prose

William Shakespeare's 1 Henry IV, aka Henry IV, Part 1: *A Retelling in Prose*

William Shakespeare's 2 Henry IV, aka Henry IV, Part 2: *A Retelling in Prose*

William Shakespeare's 1 Henry VI, aka Henry VI, Part 1: *A Retelling in Prose*

William Shakespeare's 2 Henry VI, aka Henry VI, Part 2: *A Retelling in Prose*

William Shakespeare's 3 Henry VI, aka Henry VI, Part 3: *A Retelling in Prose*

William Shakespeare's All's Well that Ends Well: *A Retelling in Prose*

William Shakespeare's Antony and Cleopatra: *A Retelling in Prose*

William Shakespeare's As You Like It: *A Retelling in Prose*

William Shakespeare's The Comedy of Errors: *A Retelling in Prose*

William Shakespeare's Coriolanus: *A Retelling in Prose*

William Shakespeare's Cymbeline: *A Retelling in Prose*

William Shakespeare's Hamlet: *A Retelling in Prose*

William Shakespeare's Henry V: *A Retelling in Prose*

William Shakespeare's Henry VIII: *A Retelling in Prose*

William Shakespeare's Julius Caesar: *A Retelling in Prose*

William Shakespeare's King John: *A Retelling in Prose*

William Shakespeare's King Lear: *A Retelling in Prose*

William Shakespeare's Love's Labor's Lost: *A Retelling in Prose*

William Shakespeare's Macbeth: *A Retelling in Prose*

William Shakespeare's Measure for Measure: *A Retelling in Prose*

William Shakespeare's The Merchant of Venice: *A Retelling in Prose*

William Shakespeare's The Merry Wives of Windsor: *A Retelling in Prose*

William Shakespeare's A Midsummer Night's Dream: *A Retelling in Prose*

William Shakespeare's Much Ado About Nothing: *A Retelling in Prose*

William Shakespeare's Othello: *A Retelling in Prose*

William Shakespeare's Pericles, Prince of Tyre: *A Retelling in Prose*

William Shakespeare's Richard II: *A Retelling in Prose*

William Shakespeare's Richard III: *A Retelling in Prose*

William Shakespeare's Romeo and Juliet: *A Retelling in Prose*

William Shakespeare's The Taming of the Shrew: *A Retelling in Prose*

William Shakespeare's The Tempest: *A Retelling in Prose*

William Shakespeare's Timon of Athens: *A Retelling in Prose*

William Shakespeare's Titus Andronicus: *A Retelling in Prose*

William Shakespeare's Troilus and Cressida: *A Retelling in Prose*

William Shakespeare's Twelfth Night: *A Retelling in Prose*

William Shakespeare's The Two Gentlemen of Verona: *A Retelling in Prose*

William Shakespeare's The Two Noble Kinsmen: *A Retelling in Prose*

William Shakespeare's The Winter's Tale: *A Retelling in Prose*